"Johnny Elbert Finlay," called out Miss Blair.

He took a deep breath and reached into his knapsack, which he had brought from his locker at lunchtime. As he drew out the root, dirt spilled on his desk. Cecil's muffled off-key humming of "Corn Likker" could be heard along with snickering and whispering. With a stern look, Miss Blair quieted them by slapping a book down on her desk.

Now it was almost too quiet. Johnny paused as he stood in front of the class. A sea of wide mimicking eyes merged to make one giant monster. That monster seemed strong enough to knock Johnny off his feet. His knees felt wobbly. His insides fluttered like Aunt Lou's chickens when a red-tailed hawk came near. At that moment, he wanted to run—all the way to Mirror Mountain. There, in a quiet hollow, he'd be away from prying eyes. But it was too late. . .

MYSTERY on MIRROR MOUNTAIN

Ask for these White Horse titles from Chariot Books:

Satch and the New Kid
Satch and the Motormouth

At Left Linebacker, Chip Demory
A Winning Season for the Braves
Mystery Rider at Thunder Ridge
Seventh Grade Soccer Star
Batter Up!
Full Court Press
A Race to the Finish

Mystery on Mirror Mountain
Courage on Mirror Mountain

A MIRROR MOUNTAIN ADVENTURE

MYSTERY
ON MIRROR MOUNTAIN

WYNNETTE FRASER

Chariot Books™
David C. Cook Publishing Co.

Chariot Books™ is an imprint of David C. Cook Publishing Co.
David C. Cook Publishing Co., Elgin, Illinois 60120
David C. Cook Publishing Co., Weston, Ontario
Nova Distribution Ltd., Torquay, England

MYSTERY ON MIRROR MOUNTAIN
© 1989 by Wynnette Fraser.

Designed by Elizabeth Thompson
Cover illustration by Wendy Wassink Ackison
Edited by Dave and Neta Jackson

First Printing, 1989
Printed in the United States of America
96 95 94 93 92 7 6 5 4 3

Library of Congress Cataloging-in-Publication Data
Fraser, Wynnette, 1925-
    Mystery on Mirror Mountain / Wynnette Fraser.
        p.   cm.—(A Mirror Mountain adventure)
    Summary: Eleven-year-old Johnny's fears about returning to school
after a three-year absence dissipate when he meets a sympathetic
teacher and makes a new friend who is interested in his life on Mirror
Mountain.
    ISBN 1-55513-588-9
    [1. Mountain life—Fiction. 2. Schools—Fiction. 3. Friendship—
Fiction. 4. Christian life—Fiction.]
I. Title.
PZ7.F8647My 1989
[Fic]—dc19   89-9757
                                                         CIP
                                                         AC

Dedicated to my husband and children:
Lawrence, Donna, Larry, Doug,
and in memory of Beth

Contents

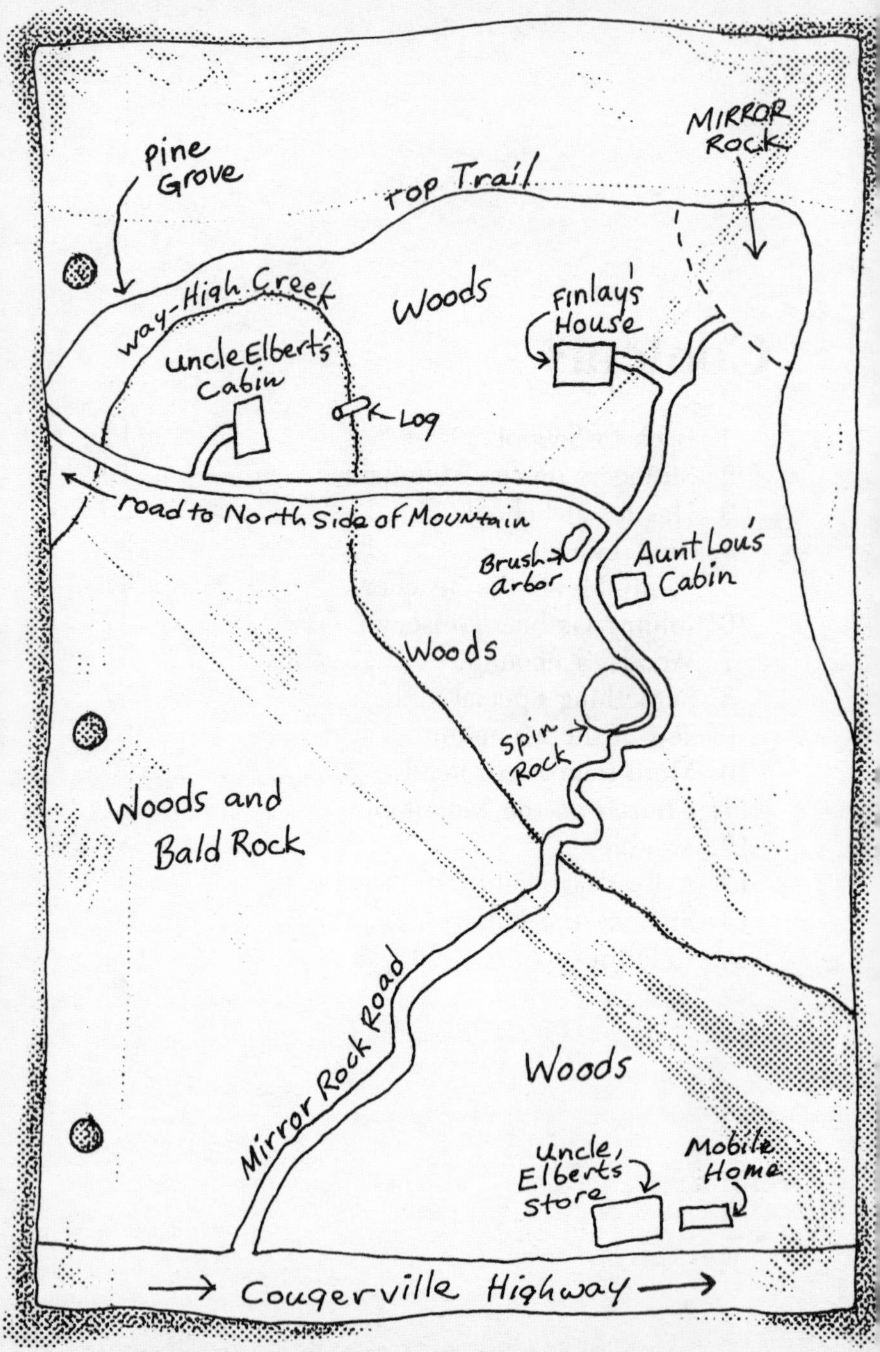

Pine Grove
Top Trail
MIRROR Rock
way-High Creek
Woods
Finlay's House
Uncle Elbert's Cabin
Log
road to North Side of Mountain
Brush Arbor
Aunt Lou's Cabin
Woods
Spin Rock
Woods and Bald Rock
Mirror Rock Road
Woods
Uncle, Elberts Store
Mobile Home
Cougerville Highway

1
Back to School

The yellow, four-wheel-drive station wagon crawled over ruts and stones as it lurched its way up the twisting mountain road. "School Bus" was painted on it in big, black letters.

Johnny Finlay heard it coming. He hated the sound. They had no right making him go to school. Mirror Mountain could teach him everything he needed to know. Hadn't Ma and Pa and Aunt Lou lived here all their life? They were doing okay. His sister, Louise, was the only one who wanted to move down to Cougarville.

Johnny pushed Midnight's black nose away and wiggled deeper into the leaves between the two old logs. The pesky dog always wanted to lick him in the face.

11

Actually, Johnny admitted to himself, Pa and Ma did have it pretty rough on the mountain. They stayed to take care of Aunt Lou, but there wasn't much a man could do to earn a living. For years Pa had made moonshine—illegal corn whiskey. Then the law caught him and sent him to prison.

When he got out, Pa promised the family that he'd never make moonshine again. He'd find some other work. And he had, too, ten miles away at Uncle Elbert's store. It was on the highway that ran past the foot of the huge granite mountain that stuck up like a giant ghost out of the almost level countryside. Every day Pa faithfully rode his dirt bike down and back. But things weren't easy.

The time he'd spend in prison must have been real hard on him. Johnny remembered the look on his father's face when they went to court about the school business. The judge had been very upset that Johnny and Louise hadn't been going down the mountain to school. No ordinary school bus had ever dared drive up the treacherous road. So when Pa's old Chevy broke down for the last time, the children had just stayed home.

"I order the county to provide a special four-wheel-drive vehicle to pick these children up for school each day that the weather permits. It's a disgrace that an eleven-year-old boy and a thirteen-year-old girl have missed three whole years of school for lack of adequate transportation. This state guarantees each child an education, and in this day and age, there's no excuse for not providing it," said the judge. Then he turned to Pa and in an even sterner voice said: "Mr. Finlay, I see by your record that you spent time in prison for moonshining. Is that correct?"

Pa had nodded.

"Then let me tell you something," continued the judge as he leaned over his bench and glared down at Pa. "If you don't cooperate fully in sending these children to school every day, I'll have you back in prison for their truancy. Is that understood?"

Pa's face looked like the gray, weathered boards on Aunt Lou's barn. "Yes, your honor. I've always wanted them to get their schoolin'. It's just that there's been no way."

"Well, now there is. So you see that they are ready!"

Louise's voice echoed up the hollow and interrupted Johnny's memories. "You better get down here, Johnny Elbert. That bus just passed the fork to Way High Creek. It'll be here any minute. You hear me?"

"I hear ya," he called, barely loud enough for her to hear. "I guess there ain't no choice," he said to Midnight as the big black dog took off after a squirrel that had ventured too far down a nearby white oak tree. "If I was to cut school, Pa would be in trouble just as much as me."

He got up from his hiding spot and sauntered on down to the road. He hadn't been really hiding—just being alone.

Johnny had his Pa's wide face and sharp hazel eyes. He was short for his age, but wiry enough to shinny up trees and run in and out of ravines like a sure-footed fox.

He spied a wild plant and carefully pulled it up by its roots. The smell of upturned leaves and damp earth joined that of Ma's fried fatback riding on the air that floated up the hollow. From a huge chestnut tree two frolicking chipmunks scolded Johnny on his way, but he wasn't worried about being late for the bus.

Just then the old dog caught up with the boy. "You hear that dumb school bus, Midnight?"

The dog whined and turned his dark head to one side. Midnight belonged to Aunt Lou, who lived a little way down the mountain. At night, he guarded her cabin. But every day at first light, he sprinted up the road and scratched on Johnny's window until he would climb out and go for a jaunt in the woods before breakfast. Now, Midnight had to wait for Johnny to dress, eat, and pack his books. There wasn't much time for a ramble.

"Don't make sense," Johnny declared, "them sending a bus up here. Even the mailman don't come up this mountain, and we only got electricity last year. But that Sandy McRee aims to come every day—rain or shine."

This was the second week of school.

The little bus arrived just as Johnny jumped down onto the road and grabbed up his books. From behind the steering wheel Sandy's warm smile covered all his lean, tanned face. Good looking and tall, his hair matched his name. Since last spring, Sandy had been the local preacher, and had been a good friend of the children. At least Johnny had considered him a friend until Sandy volunteered to drive their bus as a part-time job.

Louise returned Sandy's greeting with a wave. But Johnny merely gave a nod as he climbed into the back seat and plopped his books down between him and his sister. On top of them he put the root he'd pulled while coming out down the hollow.

Dirt and leaves clung to his T-shirt and jeans. He scowled at Louise's disapproving glance as he brushed himself off. She was tall and slender like her mother, and she had on a new dress with autumn colors that matched her eyes and long, honey-blond hair. "You brought that dirty old root on this school bus," she accused.

He looked at the spider-shaped root. It dribbled dirt and leaf-mold over his new books. He was sorry he hadn't packed them in the new knapsack Pa had bought him as a "goin' back to school" present.

"Ain't just any old root," he said. "Blue cohosh sells good to mountain women at Uncle Elbert's store." His sharp eyes squinted at the driver. "I was aiming to leave this with Aunt Lou—if Sandy'll stop there a skinny minute."

Sandy, a ministerial student at Cougarville College, glanced at his watch. "Guess so," he said, "but why not take it to school with you? Third graders still have 'show and tell,' don't they?"

Johnny's chin went up staunchly. "So what? I ain't

15

a little young'un like the rest of 'em. I'm eleven. All my old classmates have gone on up. Fact is, I'd rather stay home." A queasy feeling stabbed the pit of his stomach. It happened whenever he thought of school.

The bus moved with caution down the rock-studded road, requiring constant alertness on the part of its driver.

"I know it's not easy," Sandy said, "having to catch up after missing three years of school. It was too bad the regular bus couldn't come, and then your Pa's car quitting on him."

"Not so bad," Johnny sighed. "We was doing just fine before you come hiking up here, Sandy. I ain't again' Bible talk and praying, mind you. Aunt Lou thinks right smart of that. I'm glad for the change it done Pa, too. But going back to school..."

"I'm glad for your Pa's guitar playing at church," Sandy interrupted.

"Corn Kelly ain't pleased over none of it," Johnny said. "He's mad 'cause Pa don't help him make moonshine no more."

"Let him be," Louise put in. "Corn Kelly's the meanest man on this here mountain. His skinny little wife's so scared of him, she don't dare say she wants to go to church or anywheres. Good thing there ain't no young'uns for him to mistreat."

"Didn't you tell me they lived in that shanty down the road from your Uncle Elbert's old cabin?" Sandy asked.

Johnny nodded at Sandy's back. "Yep. That was the

same day we went fishin' up Way High Creek." His thin lips tightened. "We could be fishin' today if you hadn't started meddlin' about our schoolin'."

Louise glared at her brother. "If Sandy hadn't helped, Pa would've been thrown right back in jail."

"I hate school," Johnny declared. "I'd rather hunt herbs for Aunt Lou. She's too old to be trompin' them hollows, anyway."

"I know," Sandy said, "but you need to go to school."

"Aunt Lou never went, and she lives good off of sellin' herbs. She's teaching me how." A proud look crossed his face. "She says I'm good at figuring."

"There's more to be learned than figuring," Louise put in with a curt toss of her head. "It's high time Aunt Lou got rid of work she ain't able to do by herself no more." She shook her head, causing her long hair to flounce about her shoulders. "Having to look after Aunt Lou's what keeps us here. Else, we could live in Cougarville, and Pa and Ma'd make good money at Cougarville Textiles. We're the only family with kids that's left up here."

"Don't you go blaming Aunt Lou!" Johnny's eyes narrowed. "Ain't no school worth leaving this mountain."

"Know what you are, Johnny Elbert Finlay? You're scared!" A shadow crossed her face. "I don't like it no better than you, havin' my classmates snub me. I feel dumb being the tallest in my class, but I don't aim to be squashed down. I'm bearing in mind what Aunt Lou said after you and me went up at church."

"Didn't say nothing about school," he tossed back.

17

"Still fits. I recollect she said, 'The Lord don't come into nobody to just set down and twiddle His thumbs. We're s'posed to let Him stand up tall and strong inside us.'"

"So what? I can do that on the mountain. Who needs to rub shoulders with highfalutin' folks like that twerp, Cecil Harwood or Scott Jenkins? Ain't nothing to me if his pa owns Cougarville Textiles, neither!"

"Scott Jenkins can't be so bad," Louise peered at him. "His sister, Donna, is the one girl in my class who's always nice to everybody."

"Didn't say he was hateful," Johnny replied. "He don't make fun of people like Cecil does. It's them little kids that make me sick."

"How?"

"Acting like Scott's some kind of hero. He's big as me, and he's just eight. But they look at me like I was something the cat drug in."

Louise giggled. "Sandy don't look like no cat!"

A smile picked up the corners of Johnny's wide mouth. Sandy let out a loud "meow" from the driver's seat and laughter filled the yellow station wagon like a burst of sunshine.

2
Strangers on the Mountain

After passing the Way High Creek turn-off on their right, the little bus rounded a twisting curve and Aunt Lou's log cabin came in sight on the left side of the road.

With the toe of his boot, Sandy touched the brake. "You know," he said to Johnny, "I doubt if those little kids in your class ever heard how roots and herbs are gathered. I think you should take the root to school."

"And get laughed at? Not me. Anyhow, it needs hanging in Aunt Lou's cellar to dry. Let me out right here. I'll be back in two shakes of a dead cow's tail!"

The station wagon stopped. Johnny hopped out and darted to the porch where Aunt Lou sat. The tiny woman seemed to expect him. She had thrown a warm shawl over her slight shoulders and print dress that almost touched her ankles. Neat plaits of white hair framed her smiling face.

Before Johnny reached the porch, Midnight came streaking past him. With his long tongue flapping from the side of his mouth, the dog sidled up to Aunt Lou for an affectionate pat on the head.

Aunt Lou waved toward the bus. "Just set the root on them steps," she said to Johnny.

The dog tried to follow Johnny back to the bus.

"Go to Aunt *Lou*!" the boy commanded. He emphasized the "ooh" sound. Midnight knew what that meant but gave Johnny a long, sad look. Then the dog turned and loped back to the cabin.

The weather had been unusually dry for a whole month, but Mirror Mountain Road was still the worst in the county. Every winter, repeated onslaughts of sleet and rain chopped chasms in the red dirt. Rocks of all sizes toppled down off the bank. If a rock was too heavy, the driver was forced to find help in moving it off the road.

Spin Rock had been too heavy for any number of men to move, so the mountain people had detoured around it. After circling the big piece of granite, the little bus moved along a few yards of straight road before it reached treacherous Spin Curve.

Suddenly, without warning, two helmeted figures

on motorcycles appeared, heading straight for the bus.

Louise screamed. Sandy swerved quickly to the narrow right shoulder of the road and stopped. The motorcycle riders were moving at a fast speed. They were almost to Spin Rock before they could slow and turn around. They drove back alongside the halted bus. Both were wearing faded jeans and cut-off T-shirts.

"We're so sorry!" The speaker's bright brown eyes looked startled. A thick shock of dark red hair stuck out of his helmet. His beard was also dark red and bushy above wide, muscular shoulders.

"Thing was," he explained to Sandy, "we've seen so few cars on this road, we didn't expect any so early in the morning. You folks all right?"

Sandy breathed deeply and nodded. "Just a bit shook up. You have to be careful. Lots of places along here don't even have enough room for two to pass, and someone has to back up or go off the edge."

"It sure is a terrible road," put in the other helmeted man. Smaller than his companion, he had long, scruffy blond hair. The tenor ring in his voice matched his quiet, blue eyes. He didn't seem wild or daring.

The bearded one did, though. He boomed out a promise to be more careful. "Glad no one was hurt," he said as the motorcycles spun around and roared off up the mountain.

Johnny noticed how pleasant the men had been. Pa always said strangers acting too nice couldn't be trusted and probably had something to hide. Yet Pa was much nicer now. It was confusing to put together and would bear some thinking when he had more time.

Sandy pulled the bus back from the grassy shoulder. "That was close," he said. "Do you know those guys?"

"Maybe they're the ones who rented Uncle Elbert's old cabin about a month ago," Johnny replied. "Pa told us to stay away from them. He don't trust strangers."

Louise nudged her brother. He felt himself blush. He'd forgotten that Sandy had also been a stranger when he first met the Finlays.

Sandy didn't seem to notice. He was too busy watching the road. After awhile he said, "I didn't know your Uncle Elbert had rented out the cabin."

"He did. I heard him tell Pa he didn't like it sitting empty after he moved his family to the doublewide mobile home beside his store."

"Uncle Elbert said them strangers seemed all right to him," Louise added, "planting a garden and such." A wistful look went into her eyes. "Wish we could have a mobile home with all that shiny new stuff in it," she mused. "Cindy and Ray Arthur got such nice rooms."

Johnny didn't answer. A firecracker had exploded in his mind. The ginseng patch! Year after year, in an isolated hollow in the rich woods near Way High Creek, he had harvested plants for Aunt Lou. Its location was a family secret, but Uncle Elbert's cabin was near by. What if the strangers found it? Would they know how valuable the herb was?

I got to get up there, thought Johnny. The larger plants might even be ready to gather by now. If only he didn't have to go to school, he could be up there digging them this very minute. The old queasy feeling tightened his stomach again.

3
Hassles at School

When Johnny and Louise stepped out of the station wagon at Cougarville Elementary School, the bell had already rung. Sandy scribbled notes to explain their tardiness to the teachers.

Johnny didn't mind being late. That way, only the home room pupils would get a chance to stare at him. No sneers or taunts would echo across the big school yard; no corny mountain songs announcing his arrival.

Miss Blair was writing in her roll book. Her light brown hair framed her face with soft curls; her blue eyes were fixed on the book. She wasn't much taller than Johnny was, and he liked the way she looked. Today, she wore a lavender dress, which made her eyes look almost violet.

Johnny crept into the room. His hair still fell across his short, wide forehead. His steps, so sure when he ran in and out of mountain ravines, were now cautious and slow.

Halfway down the aisle, a foot shot out. He stumbled over it. To steady himself, he grasped the edge of a desk, which moved under the weight of his hand. The next moment, his head and shoulders were sprawled over the top of the desk. He turned to face its occupant. Two wide blue eyes met his own. They belonged to Betty Lou Haskell, a shy little girl with light blonde hair.

"S'cuse me," he stammered. He felt the pinkness rush to his face as he righted himself. The other children laughed; Miss Blair looked up. Faces straightened.

"You're late, Johnny," Miss Blair said.

"Yes'm. I got a note." He took it to her. His new sneakers squeaked and left little crumbles of mountain earth on the pale yellow linoleum.

Once he was back at his desk, Johnny cast his sharp hazel eyes about to see who had tripped him.

Willis Thompson could have done it. He was in the right place. Willis's weak eyes peered through thick glasses topped by dark bangs. Whatever question the teacher asked, his hand always went up. No, Johnny decided; it wasn't Willis. He might be a know-it-all, but he sure wasn't brave enough.

Cecil Harwood was a different story. He looked smug as he sat across the aisle from Willis — too smug and innocent. Cecil would trip his own grandmother for a laugh. In two days, Johnny had figured that out. He glared at the boy. Straight red hair and green eyes. *Looks like a Christmas tree*, thought Johnny. But Cecil had no gifts hanging on his scrawny branches. Johnny knew he could lick the mouthy little pest with one hand. He wouldn't, though. He was bigger and older, and it would never pass as a fair fight. It was enough to be called "mountain boy"; he'd give no one reason to pin "bully" on him, too. There had to be another way to even the score.

"Johnny, did you hear me?" Miss Blair's voice broke into his thoughts. "Get out your math workbook," she said.

He obeyed, glad to put his mind on the one school subject he liked. His teacher was as nice as she was pretty. It wasn't her fault that he hated school; he wanted to please her.

Johnny didn't look forward to recess. Not that he was left out of games. The teachers who supervised playtime tried to make certain all of the children were included. But for Johnny, that took something away from being asked. He longed to be with his cousin, but Ray Arthur, Uncle Elbert's son, was with his own sixth grade classmates. They used another part of the playground at recess. Just playing with boys his own size might help, thought Johnny. That way, he could fight back any of the boys who sneaked kicks, bites, or jabs at him when the teacher wasn't looking. Cecil Harwood always seemed to get them started by humming some "corn likker" mountain tune.

Not everyone listened to Cecil, though. Scott Jenkins was only eight and a half, but he was taller and stronger than anyone in third grade. Scott's dark, brown hair shone with good health; his tanned face made his straight teeth look whiter than they would, otherwise. Sharp brown eyes seemed to say "I like you" to Johnny. But Scott was the mill owner's son and the brightest boy in the class. Nobody jostled Scott or pushed him around. That was because he was rich, Johnny decided. Scott didn't need to act nice to be treated well. So why did he bother? How would Johnny Elbert Finlay act if his parents weren't poor? He wondered.

Third grade reading class didn't go well. Johnny stumbled through paragraphs he had to read aloud. The more words he missed, the more his mind refused to work. The other children wiggled with impatience and snickered.

"I'd like to put you in the fourth grade, Johnny," Miss Blair had said, "but you don't read well enough yet." Then she seemed to notice his face growing red as it did every time he had to read before the class.

"We'll get extra help for you," she promised. "You really are super in math, Johnny."

That made him feel better. "I learned that on the mountain," he said with pride in his voice.

Miss Blair smiled as if she understood. Johnny liked the way her smile started by lighting up her eyes, then spreading over her soft face till dimples punctuated each cheek.

"It must be beautiful on the mountain," she said.

"It is," Johnny agreed. "If you ain't been on Mirror Mountain, you ain't been nowhere."

"Anywhere," she corrected.

Johnny let that stand. "We get all the TV stations with no antenna." A whispered "wow!" prodded him on. "And when there's no clouds, you can almost see the ocean!"

"No way!" Cecil Harwood hooted. "He's putting us on!"

Miss Blair smiled again. "Well, it must seem that way when you look at things from such a high elevation. Johnny's fortunate to live on Mirror Mountain."

"I'd love to live up there," Scott Jenkins put in. Johnny saw Cecil Harwood and Willis Thompson exchange smirky glances.

When the bell rang, Scott came over and walked out with Johnny.

"I collect rocks and arrowheads," Scott said. "Do you have many of them on your mountain?"

"All kinds of that stuff and more," Johnny bragged.

"Would you help me hunt them some Saturday?"

"Sure. If you can get up there, I'll take you all over that mountain. It's a bad road going up, though."

"I'll talk to Dad, and you ask your parents, too."

"Better come before frost sets in. It's gonna get cold up there."

"If Dad and Mother let me come, would this Saturday be all right?" Scott's eyes were eager, expectant.

29

Johnny felt a flutter inside him as he agreed to ask his folks.

Cecil and Willis, who walked just ahead of them, were too quiet, as if trying to hear the conversation.

"Come on, Scott," urged Cecil in a loud voice. "You gonna waste all day talking to that mountain boy? He'll have you eating snake eggs before you know it!"

Scott moved forward. With the quickness of a disturbed wildcat, he grabbed Cecil's ear. "You watch yourself!" he cautioned. "Keep talking like that and I'll twist your ear off. You'd better learn to show other people some respect!"

"I . . . I was just kidding," Cecil howled. Willis' eyes widened as he stepped out of the way.

Scott released the smaller boy. Cecil's face was pale. Just as Johnny had thought, the little twerp was mostly mouth and no courage. Suddenly, he didn't feel so alone any more.

"See you tomorrow," he said to Scott as the yellow station wagon rolled up in the school driveway.

Louise couldn't believe Johnny's news. "One of them rich Jenkinses? What'll they think of our awful looking house!"

"Scott ain't coming to look at our house. He wants to hunt rocks and arrowheads."

"You're counting chickens before they hatch," his sister informed. "Scott's Ma and Pa ain't likely to let him come up there."

"And just why not, Miss Smarty?"

"'Cause they probably know Pa was jailed for

30

bootlegging."

"Pa ain't makin' no more moonshine," he reminded her.

"The Jenkinses might not believe that," Louise suggested.

"I'd give them the benefit of the doubt," Sandy put in. "Anyhow, the idea of Scott visiting sounds great to me."

Johnny made a silly face at his sister. She stuck out her tongue then ignored him to stare gloomily out of the window. A shadow of uncertainty crossed her face.

In his rear view mirror, Sandy noticed. "How did your day go, Louise?" He asked.

"All right, I guess," She sighed wearily.

"Only all right? Why not better?"

She clamped her lips together in a tight line. When she spoke, her voice quivered. "There's too much to learn. Them boys and girls in my class laugh at how I talk."

"Oh?" Sandy said. "I suppose your way of talking is a bit different, Louise. But it's natural for you and gives *me* no problem. Yet I know children can be cruel to someone who's different in any way at all."

"Humph. There's others different 'sides me. The black children got their way and the Vietnamese just know a few words of English. Nobody laughs at them."

"Just give yourself and the others more time. As you read and practice speaking correctly, they'll stop noticing."

"That ain't fast enough," she said weakly. She

brushed her long hair from her face. From the pocket of her gold paisley dress, she dug out a tissue to blot her moist eyes and cheeks.

Why did girls always have to cry, thought Johnny.

When they reached the clearing, Sandy stopped the bus and turned to Louise. "Hey, now," he said gently, "nobody said catching up would be easy or quick. Seems I heard you telling Johnny something about being strong this very morning."

"Yeah!" Johnny remembered. "Now, who ain't letting God stand up tall?"

"We all have trouble doing that," Sandy reminded him. "Let's just ask for some extra strength before Johnny and I start back downhill."

It was a short prayer, but Johnny felt better afterwards. After setting his books on the rock, he hopped in beside Sandy to ride back down the mountain as far as Aunt Lou's cabin.

Louise waved as they drove off. She was smiling.

4
Aunt Lou

Since Pa worked till dark each day, Johnny was Aunt Lou's only helper with outside chores. In addition to her wild herb business, the plucky little woman had a garden, chickens, and a cow named Bossy. Ma and Louise helped with canning and freezing, but Pa said outside jobs belonged to the men of the family.

On the porch of her log cabin, Aunt Lou watched forkfuls of fresh-baked apple pie disappear in her great nephew's mouth. Between bites, Johnny told her about Scott wanting to visit him. Pleasure lights glowed in Aunt Lou's hazel eyes and crinkles tightened around her smile.

"I'll fix lunch for your hike," she offered.

Johnny grinned approval. "We'll hit Way High Creek

about noon," he said. "I know a good place to hunt arrowheads." His smiled faded. "Louise says the Jenkinses might not let Scott come if they know about Pa's moonshinin' days with Corn Kelly."

A little frown crossed her face. "Grant it, your Pa was wrong to ever get messed up with that no 'count Corn," she said, "even if there ain't much a man can do to make a living for his family on this here mountain." Her balled fists rested on her small, bony knees. "But bootleggin's contrary to the laws of God and man." Her proud chin pushed her head up and down. "No mind now—he's paid his dues. God forgived him and people ought to do the same."

"Pa's doing real good now, ain't he?" said Johnny.

"Mighty right he is. It's all of the Lord's pouring some sense in him."

"Louise thinks he oughta get a better job," Johnny offered.

Aunt Lou shook her head. "It's hard to get a job without learnin' this day and time. Till now, no Finlay's had more'n a year or two of schoolin'. Now, your Grandma Finlay—she was downright smart. No telling how far she'd have gone if she'd had the chance you young'uns got."

"I don't like school," Johnny stated.

Aunt Lou was so short, she had to stand to look down at him. Hands on hips, she had the look of a wildcat about to strike.

"Listen here, Johnny Elbert Finlay! I'd give my right arm to be in your place. Lord knows, it was hard enough getting a bus up here for you young'uns. You ain't trying to tell me you're hatching up ideas for throwing your chance away?"

When Aunt Lou's words flashed the way her eyes did, no one argued with her. Johnny had held the last forkful of apple pie in mid-air till she finished. Now, he slid the morsel into his wide mouth and swallowed it whole. He sighed. "I'll go to school, Aunt Lou."

"Then all's settled," she said in a quieter voice. "I got some figuring for you to do."

A few minutes later, Johnny determined that Aunt Lou cleared $225 from August herb shipments to a pharmaceutical firm in Asheville. Then she remembered another $100 from sales at Uncle Elbert's store. In her orange composition book, Johnny recorded the total: $325.

Aunt Lou brought out the mail order catalog. He wrote as she called out items and numbers: piece goods for winter sewing; new jeans, shirts, and a pocket knife for Johnny. She insisted he had earned it.

"Now take that book home tonight and tell Louise to write in something pretty for herself. Girls got their own ideas." She paused a moment, then noticed how low the sun hung above a big chestnut tree at the end of the yard.

"Curling rattlesnakes!" she exclaimed. "It's past time to milk Bossy."

Johnny rose and put the catalog on a bench. "I'll fetch her from the pasture," he said.

"No need," Aunt Lou said. "She's bound to be wait-

35

ing out back. That cow can tell time better'n you or I." She followed him down the steps. "You go feed the chickens and gather eggs while I tend to the milkin'."

Midnight popped up from his dozing place on the bottom step and ran ahead of them. In front of the barn, he leaped into the middle of a host of squawking chickens. Johnny followed the path the dog had created. Just inside the door, he fed three or four ears of dry corn into the sheller. As he turned the crank, golden grains spattered against the inside of the sheller box. He tossed them to the restless chickens.

Soft breezes played through the pines, causing the needles to make a whishing sound as they brushed against each other.

Johnny took a deep breath. The air was good to smell; barn odors mixed with pungent pine. Everything seemed so right at Aunt Lou's. He liked the way his hands moved to get chores done, the way his brain stayed in place. It was as if his lean young body had been set down like the oaks that grew so well on the mountain. No better place to grow, he thought.

The roar of motors on the mountain road broke his moment of quietness. Soon came the "varoom" as the two motorcycles passed Aunt Lou's; then a slowing down sound, and finally the whining pick-up as the motorcyclists took the left fork to Uncle Elbert's cabin.

Why had the stangers come to the mountain? They had seemed concerned over the near accident that morning. Maybe they were all right, but there was the ginseng patch. What if they stumbled on it and tried

36

to harvest the plants? He'd not mention that possibility to Aunt Lou. No need for her to worry. No, he'd just have to get those big plants dug before something like that happened. It was true, the ginseng was on government land, but mountain diggers had a code of ethics: once someone re-seeded a patch, others could tell and they left it alone. Outsiders wouldn't know or care about ethics. He wished for a fence around Mirror Mountain, the kind that shut out strangers.

After he had gathered eggs and thrown some hay down from the loft for Bossy, Aunt Lou sent Johnny home with a fresh pat of butter on top of the catalog. "That's enough to carry," she decided. "Eggs and milk can go, next passing."

He gave Midnight a goodbye hug and headed home. When he reached the clearing, the smell of Ma's scorched grits greeted his nostrils. He made a disappointed little face. If only Ma cooked as well as Aunt Lou. He'd said as much to his great aunt, but she reminded him that Ma wasn't well.

Pa had another explanation. He said Ma's mind was on the corn shuck mats and willow baskets he had to haul down to Uncle Elbert's store to sell for her. Yet Pa seemed proud of how gifted Ma was with her hands. He made it a weekly contest between them as to which sold best—Ma's crafts or the honey from his beegums. He had five of them lined up under two sourwood trees at the back of the clearing. Everyone said Pa was the best beekeeper on the mountain. If

Ma won the contest, Pa said "thanks for the burnt grits." When his honey sold best, Ma said he pushed those shiny golden jars out in front of everything else. After that, the two usually laughed and hugged each other. Johnny and Louise couldn't tell that either of them was the loser.

Such light-hearted times were better than when Pa and Corn Kelly used to draw a new batch of moonshine in some hidden ravine. New moonshine had to be tested, Pa would insist in a wobbly voice that was too loud. Ma's face would darken as Pa found fault with her cooking; Johnny and Louise went to their rooms. Sadness would stick to their spirits like leeches. It was hard to realize that was less than a year ago.

With the sunset on his back, Johnny stopped at the big rock. He set the catalog and butter on his books then picked up the whole stack. Moving slowly to balance his load, he entered the house and plopped the books down on the big oak dining table.

In the room where the family lived and ate meals, a small black and white TV set was going strong. The evening news was on. A reporter's voice came from behind a helicopter that whirred across the screen. "Illegal marijuana crops have become a major problem in the area," he said. "Law enforcement officers are kept busy trying to locate and destroy isolated patches."

"Move that stuff off the table!" Louise's bossy command annoyed his ears.

"Part of it's for you," he informed her. "Aunt Lou's

making up a mail order."

His sister avoided his pleased grin and picked up the catalog with the plastic bag of butter on top. "This here butter oughta be in the refrigerator," she said as she sidled through the door to the kitchen. Johnny shrugged his shoulders and moved his books.

After supper, he went to his room to study. As he sat on the many-colored quilt that covered his cot, his eyes wandered over the room. On shelves Pa had built on one wall, his clean clothes were neatly folded. Several hooks held the hang-up clothes. Except for the bright quilt, it was a drab room. A coat of paint was needed everywhere except on the thin plywood partition behind the cot. Pa had built that, too, so each of the children could have a private room. The partition split the room between two windows. On her side of the partition, Louise had hung an extra quilt that matched the one on her cot. "Cuts down all the racket you and Midnight make when you leave on them early morning rambles," she'd said.

He propped a pillow behind him and opened his reading book. If only he could sound out words as quickly as he caught on to math problems, but it didn't seem possible.

The sound of Pa's guitar drifted in from the front room, soft and smooth. The notes fell quietly on Johnny's ear and filled him with the feeling that all was well.

Pa and Ma had said that of course, Scott could visit. Would the Jenkinses let him come? And if he came, would Scott be disappointed and even sorry for how the Finlays lived? Johnny had longed for a friend his own age, someone to share the fun he had on the mountain. Since Uncle Elbert had picked up and moved his family beside the highway store, Johnny had missed Ray Arthur. He only saw him at church once a week. Uncle Elbert's family seldom missed Sandy McRee's outdoor services. But Uncle Elbert never hung around long after church. "Ain't safe to leave a store for thieves to break in and steal," he'd say in a Bible-quoting way. That always cut short the fun the boys might have.

Johnny was glad Aunt Lou had suggested the picnic lunches. That way, he wouldn't have to risk Ma forgetting and burning a meal while Scott was there. He wouldn't want her to be embarrassed over something like that.

5
Sandy Meets the Teacher

Each morning that week, Sandy McRee had let Johnny and Louise hop out of the bus in front of the school. Then he would hurry on to his college classes. But not today. After making certain the children were on foot, he guided the yellow station wagon to a vacant parking space and parked the vehicle.

Johnny noticed, and started to go over to ask why. At that point, Louise pressed the toe of his sneaker with one of her penny-loafered feet.

"Ow!" he exclaimed. "How come you did that? I was just gonna ask why. . . ."

"It ain't none of your business or he'd have told you," his sister clipped. "Keep your mouth shut and your eyes open!"

He studied Louise's warning glance for a moment before they went separate ways, then shrugged. "Who cares, anyway," he muttered.

Johnny's face and lips smarted in the crisp, dry air. He coughed. Even in times of drought, the breezes that flitted around Mirror Mountain held some moisture. But down here it was dryer than strung-up leather britches beans. He headed for the water fountain, but kept an eye on Sandy.

The tall young man strode across the school yard, shoulders straight and high. Johnny didn't miss the way the female teachers standing near the school's green door, turned their heads toward Sandy. The young man went straight to the group of teachers, and Johnny could tell he was introducing himself to them.

Then it looked like Sandy singled out Miss Blair. The two of them moved away from the other teachers and talked. They smiled at each other a lot, and Johnny wished he could read lips. It hit him that their conversation might concern him. Maybe he shouldn't have said all he had to Sandy about hating school. He shot a glance toward Louise, whose steady gaze was fixed on the couple. Johnny figured his sister was also trying to read lips.

"Hi, Johnny!"

He whirled around toward the voice. Scott Jenkins looked great in navy blue pants and sweater vest over a red checked shrt. He turned to wave at the driver of a big, blue car as it pulled out of the driveway. Then the brown-haired boy strolled over to Johnny.

"Mom and Dad said I could come Saturday, if it's all right with your folks!" Scott's dark eyes were bright with excitement.

"Well, it sure is," Johnny said, his grin spreading all over his short, wide face.

"My mom and dad weren't sure at first," the younger boy said. "Then I told them Sandy McRee drove your school bus, and guess what!"

Johnny waited.

"Dad knows Sandy," Scott went on. "Sandy worked at the mill part-time last year." Scott bent over the fountain and pressed the button. A shower of water washed up against his lips, and he licked them dry. "Dad didn't tell me that, though. I heard him talking to Sandy on the phone."

"What'd they say?"

"He asked Sandy if it was safe for me to visit you on the mountain." Scott shrugged. "My folks still treat me like a little kid, you know."

"What'd Sandy tell him?"

"I just heard one side of it. But I kept out of sight and listened when Dad talked with Mom after he hung up the phone." He drank from the fountain again and blotted his moist lips with his shirtsleeve. "Dad told Mom that Sandy said he'd been going up there for a year or more. He said he was sure I'd be safer there than lots of places."

"Was that all?" The look on Scott's face told Johnny it wasn't.

"Not quite. Mom 'er. . .asked about the moonshin-in.'" Scott bit his lip as a shadow went over Johnny's wide face. "Well, you know that big mouth, Cecil. My mom heard it from his mom."

"Reckon that figures."

"Well, Dad told her that Sandy told him Mr. Finlay had put the Lord in charge of his life and didn't make or drink the stuff any more. He said Sandy said your Aunt Lou was priceless."

"Sure ain't nobody else like her," Johnny said proudly.

"Then Dad told Mom it might do the Harwoods some good if they went up to hear Sandy preach sometime."

Johnny grinned. "Ain't gonna help nobody unless they left Cecil at home."

"You've got to learn how to handle Cecil," Scott said. "My Mom says his parents don't spend much time with him. She says he shows off to get attention."

"If he keeps a'pestering me, he's gonna get more attention than he can handle." Johnny made a ball with his fist.

The door nearest their homeroom was painted orange. As the two boys walked toward it, Johnny shot a glance at Sandy and Miss Blair. Sandy's big shoulders were level with her eyes; she had to look up to talk to him.

When she entered the classroom a few minutes later, Miss Blair's blue eyes sparkled above her flushed

44

cheeks. There was a breathless excitement about her as she organized her desk to begin the day. Wisps of light brown curls framed her face, and Johnny thought that she looked downright pretty.

Sandy seemed pleased when Johnny told him about Scott's plans to visit on the mountain. The little station wagon moved more smoothly on the afternoon climb. "And what else happened at school today?" he wanted to know.

"Ummmm—let me see." Johnny scratched his head. "Cecil Harwood started a'humming 'Corn Likker.' Miss Blair didn't notice at first." He watched the back of Sandy's tanned neck turn red. Pleased at the young man's reaction, Johnny kept going. "It was like her mind was somewheres else all day long. But when she heard Cecil, she flew all over him." He caught his breath. "She said if she heard any more humming, the person doin' it would stay in at recess."

Sandy chuckled. "Guess that stopped it, eh?"

"Till recess. Wish she'd caught him and kept him in." Johnny clamped his lips together in a tight line. "I just don't know how come she gave us that social studies 'signment, though."

Sandy said nothing. This, Johnny had not expected.

"You wanting to know what it was?" He craned his short neck toward the driver's seat.

"You might as well tell us," Louise cut in from behind him. "That mouth of yours ain't stopped since we got on this here bus."

He turned to fix his sister with a quick bad face.

45

"We all got to bring something from home's what it is. It's gotta be something that ain't likely to be in everybody else's house or yard."

"No problem for you," Sandy said. "Just take the root you left at Aunt Lou's yesterday."

Johnny sat back with a sigh. "Ain't a-hankering to take nothin' at all," he declared wearily, "much less stand before the class and tell about it."

"Then how come you're making so much over it?" Louise asked.

"'Cause I ain't wanting to do it. Maybe Miss Blair'll forget. She was scatterbrained all day." He aimed a mischievous look at Sandy. "Don't see how nobody can be that happy at school!"

"Is your seat belt still fastened?" Sandy asked.

Johnny slid back and re-fastened the clip. A devilish twinkle in his eye met and danced with one in Louise's.

6
Johnny Gathers Ginseng

Johnny sat on Aunt Lou's front porch and slowly devoured a biscuit soaked with Pa's sourwood honey. On a rustic bench in front of them, Great Grandma Finlay's herb notebook lay open. In it were sketches of herbs found on the mountain.

"Not like Sandy to miss passin' the time of day, at least," Aunt Lou remarked.

"He's been in a hurry all day," Johnny said. "Reckon he had to keep a-moving." He held back a giggle as he remembered Sandy's flushed neck at the mention of Miss Blair's name. It was though he had pushed a button. For a moment, he had enjoyed a sense of power.

A drop of honey oozed from the biscuit onto his fingers. Johnny licked it off. "I ain't settled about taking no root to school," he informed Aunt Lou. He leaned forward to get a better look at the notebook.

"I can't think of nothing more interestin' to people that's never knowed about wild herbs," said Aunt Lou. She peered through her magnifying glass at the sketches.

"I ain't about to explain what blue cohosh's used for," Johnny declared.

"No, I agree that ain't the proper one to take. Sang's what sells best. Folks say it cures most any ailments — even them what ain't been named yet. The right name's 'ginseng.' That's a good one to talk about." She moistened her finger and flipped the page. "Now, this here's a good drawing, but you need the real root," she said, pointing to a sketch. "Our patch up near Way High Creek oughta be ripe for digging right now!"

An uneasy feeling stabbed Johnny's stomach. "I know, but there ain't time to go there today. Chores'll take till dark."

Aunt Lou grinned, showing all of her store-bought teeth. "Not today," she said. "Your Pa got off early and done them for you. Then he took the grass blade home with him."

"To cut grass? Pa don't never see need to do that. He says it just makes it grow too fast."

"Well, he sure did have in mind using it. Reckon

48

it's got something to do with the mill owner's young'un coming to visit. Your Pa's got more caring since Elbert counts on him right smart. Being needed perks a man up, puts pride in him. He said to me, 'Aunt Lou, I gotta clean up 'round that yard.'"

Johnny doubted his Pa had said that. The whole thing was probably Aunt Lou's idea. No matter. The yard would look better when Scott visited.

In the barn, Johnny chose one of several satchels that hung by their straps on big nails. Aunt Lou called them "haverpokes." She had sewn them from striped pillow ticking.

"Ain't nothing better to tote roots in," she said. "They don't get so skint up in them cloth bags."

Johnny flung one over his shoulder, and waved at Aunt Lou as he and Midnight headed up the road.

They took the left fork that led to the north side of the mountain. Johnny was comfortable in his short-sleeved T-shirt, for the air was still warm. Little fingers of breeze lifted wiry strands of light brown hair from his neck as he walked. The woods glowed gold and crimson, yet even the maidenhair ferns looked thirsty. No rain had fallen for a month.

Midnight darted off the road to check movements on the forest floor. As Johnny came to them, he called names of various trees aloud: "Ash, hickory, basswood, oak, maple, gum, buckeye!" He pretended Scott was beside him. He hoped his new friend would be impressed that Johnny could identify trees. At this elevation, he could point with pride to the strong, healthy plant life that existed. Higher up, some unknown disease had killed many of the trees. Johnny hoped the malady wouldn't spread downward.

He took a shortcut and crossed the creek on a big log. Midnight swam across. The dog shook his wet black hair with vigor as he stood in patches of warm sunlight that filtered through the trees. Then he rubbed himself against a myrtle bush to dry.

The ginseng patch hugged a moist, wooded slope. Several poplar and basswood trees shaded most of the area. The spot was hidden from the eyes of anyone who might walk the beaten trail through the woods.

When Johnny arrived, he let his eyes move over the patch for a moment. It appeared to be undisturbed. His wide mouth stretched out in a glad grin.

Midnight streaked off after a rabbit. Tiny dots of sunlight tagged his back as Johnny picked from the largest plants, clusters of crimson berries. He put them in his pocket, then cleared away the leaves from a big plant. To get a firm hold, he scratched around its base. Slowly, he pulled the main parts of the root from the soil.

The root didn't resist Johnny's gentle pull; fallen leaves had kept the ground soft and airy. He slid the root into his haverpoke and went on to the next plant. Five roots were enough to fill the satchel.

Johnny stood up, took the berries from his pocket, and tossed them all over the places from which he had taken the plants. "S'long, little bitty seeds," he said. "I'll see you again when you're all growed up!"

7
Woodsy Encounters

As Johnny climbed from a ravine onto the trail, Midnight's bark slashed through the air with a warning growl in it.

In the long shadows of trees, two figures moved up the path. As they drew near, Johnny recognized the motorcycle riders. He held out his hand to quiet the dog. It worked. Midnight scampered off again.

"Hi!" The voice of the bearded young man was friendly. Each of them carried two large buckets.

"You must be one of the Finlays," the bearded one went on. "We didn't get around to introductions yesterday morning. I'm Rusty, and my buddy here is Hank."

They set the buckets down, with good reason. The metal pails were full of water. Johnny eyed them and then the men, with a puzzled look.

"Guess you wonder why the water haul." Hank's voice was quieter than his companion's. "We planted some trees on the mountaintop. We're trying to save them from the drought." He paused. "And what do we call you?"

"Johnny Elbert Finlay. I never heard of nobody planting trees on this here mountain before."

The two young men exchanged glances. "It's an experiment," Rusty stated. His dark eyes had crimson specks to match the beard; and white teeth glistened when he smiled. It wasn't easy to see him as a stranger Johnny was supposed to avoid.

"We're up here to study the forest," Hank explained. Without the helmet, his long blond hair looked almost white. He had a slender face that was pink from too much sun. "I guess you knew something was killing the trees on top of the mountain."

Johnny nodded. At the moment, he wasn't thinking of the trees. He was too busy hoping the men kept to the trail, and it was obvious that they probably wouldn't. If they left it now, they would stumble on the ginseng patch.

"We'd better move on up," Rusty said. He reached to pick up his water buckets. "See you around, Johnny!"

They didn't leave the trail. With a sigh of relief, he watched them disappear around a curve. Was Pa right not to trust the men? Or was it just a habit Pa hadn't fully shed, a leftover from his moonshinin' days? The men did dress like "hippies," but they seemed and talked all right. Unless the talk about studying the forest was just a cover-up for their real reason for being on the mountain! A match struck in Johnny's brain. He might find the truth at the cabin! Pa had just said, "stay away from the strangers." He had not actually said Johnny couldn't go to the cabin when the men weren't there.

Johnny had noticed the motorcycles could be heard leaving the mountain on Saturday mornings. While they were away, he and Scott could check the cabin.

Johnny whistled, and Midnight came bounding through the bushes to join him on the way back to Way High Creek.

By the time they reached the log crossing, the sun had slid out of sight. There was a moist, woodsy smell in the air that rose from the creek.

"Rihhhpt!" The source of the sound was less than a foot from where Johnny stood. Quick as the flick of a squirrel's tail, Johnny reached down and swooped up a big, fat bullfrog. He dropped it in his pocket. Midnight ran up to sniff the quivering pocket, then backed off.

Johnny grinned. "I got plans for this here frog," he told the dog.

Suddenly Midnight's thick hairs bristled. Johnny knew his growl wasn't for the frog. The dog's nostrils had picked up another smell; Johnny spun around. Corn Kelly's beady, bloodshot eyes glared right at him.

The big man loomed over Johnny, his long crooked

nose pointing at the boy like that of a hound that had treed a coon.

"You been talkin' to yourself, Johnny Elbert Finlay?" Corn's stained beard moved grotesquely as he chomped tobacco. Johnny drew back as the man turned his unkempt head less than an inch to spit into the creek. Yellowish-brown juice made a little bubble on the water. Tiny minnows fanned out in protest.

"What's that ol' man of yours doing these days, now that he got religion?"

"Working," Johnny answered. He had never liked Corn. He hated to admit it, even to himself, but the big man frightened him, especially when he was drinking. Corn had been angry when Pa quit moonshinin'.

"You're a far piece from home," Corn said. "What's in the bag?"

"Just herbs." Johnny climbed on the log and started across. Again, Midnight splashed through the creek.

"It ain't safe 'round here with them strangers in the woods," Corn called after him.

Johnny didn't answer. He was halfway across the creek when he felt the log quivering. He knew his weight hadn't caused it; the log was strong and sturdy. As he crouched on hands and knees to steady himself, a raspy guffaw from the bank behind him, scratched the air. He turned his head to see Corn move away from the bank.

"Wobbly log!" Corn bellowed.

"Ain't so, less'n somebody wobbles it." Johnny cut back when he was safe on the other side of the creek.

Corn's malicious laughter sat like ice on Johnny's eardrums as he hurried home through the woods. For a moment, he imagined that he was four years old again. He remembered playing beneath a big chestnut in a clearing when Corn had sneaked up from behind. Without warning, the big man had jerked up the terrified boy and hoisted him over his head. "Gonna drop yer—gonna drop yer," the big monster of a man hissed through tobacco-stained teeth. Pa was angry and ordered Corn to put Johnny down.

A shiver went over Johnny now as he remembered how he had run to the house, screaming. How had Pa put up with Corn all those years? The two men weren't one bit alike.

When he reached the clearing, a warm, safe feeling rushed into Johnny and squeezed out the bad memories. Dusk was falling, so Midnight jogged down the road toward Aunt Lou's cabin.

At the door, Louise handed a pail of dirty scrub water to him.

"Least you can do," she clipped, "being it's your company that's a-comin' Saturday."

He dumped the water on Ma's marigolds and followed his sister inside. The churning in his stomach had been replaced by a good, hungry feeling. He had caught a whiff of porkchops cooking, and tonight, Ma hadn't burned them.

8
Something Special

On Friday morning, the school ground was alive with playful activity and noise. Everyone was looking forward to no school for two days. As Johnny strolled past a group of boys shooting marbles, he whistled a catchy tune.

"Hey, listen to that!" Cecil Harwood's sneerful voice matched his face. "The mountain boy whistles. Is that a 'show and tell' snake you got in that sack, Mountain Boy?"

Cecil's eyes were on the grocery bag with its top twisted; not the bulging knapsack strapped to Johnny's back. Sparks of mischief danced in Johnny's hazel eyes.

"Now, ain't you smart, Cecil," Johnny said, "a-guessing my secrets right off."

"That's not hard to do," Cecil snapped. Then he turned to the other boys and shrugged. "Not much else up there to bring but snakes, unless he's got some of his old man's moonshine in that bag!"

Johnny felt anger rip through him like buckshot at the cackling laughter that followed, but he didn't let himself think about it.

"You don't ruffle me none," Johnny drawled. "If I had a mind to, I could lay you flatter'n a hoecake with one hand, Cecil Harwood." He made a fist with his free hand. "It just ain't worth the trouble. A young'un like you's too easy to whip."

"Yeah, yeah, yeah!" Cecil jeered. "Mountain Boy's chicken!" Hoots, cackles and jeers sounded from the group.

"Want to see how chicken I am?" Johnny held out the bag at arm's length and shook it. The brown paper rattled as something moved inside.

Cecil's eyes widened. "A snake? You wouldn't dare bring a snake to school, Johnny Finlay!" His face paled as he backed away from Johnny.

"Why not?" Johnny patted his foot and cocked his head to one side. "My Pa don't make moonshine no more, and you done said there ain't nothing else I could bring from the mountain but snakes."

He bared his teeth and wrinkled up his nose as he moved toward Cecil. Then, with a quick twist, he opened the bag and up ended it, spreading the opening right over Cecil's head.

Cecil shrieked like a girl as he pawed at it, trying

to tear it off. The big bullfrog wiggled out and bounced off Cecil's chest, then landed in some shrubbery nearby. Loud whoops of laughter rose from onlookers.

"Y-you low-down, sneaking M-mountain Boy!" Cecil stammered as he backed away. Then, seeing how alone he was, his face went from white to pink to angry red. "I-I knew it was a frog all the time," he declared in a loud, whiny voice.

From a window near them, Miss Blair had watched. Johnny saw an amused smile cross her face just before she slipped out of sight.

Scott arrived as the bell was ringing. One of the other boys told him how Johnny had tricked Cecil, and the children entered the classroom in a jovial mood.

Social studies was postponed until after lunch because the class had a visitor. Betty Lou Haskell's mother brought a puppet to talk to the class about taking care of their bodies. (Betty Lou was the shy blonde girl whose desk Johnny had stumbled over the day before.)

The puppet was funny to look at, and talked about eating junk food three times a day. That, declared Joe, the puppet, was his own steady diet. "And I also think it's cool to smoke pot," Joe added.

"No, Joe!" Mrs. Haskell exclaimed. She told the puppet how marijuana messed up people's minds; how it led them to use worse drugs until nothing else mattered. Johnny had seen movies on TV about that.

"Remember," Mrs. Haskell said before she left,

"you're the only guard who's always there to care for your body. If someone offers you drugs, say 'no' and tell your parents or your teacher about it."

Johnny looked at his strong, lean arms. No drugs would ever cause him trouble. Not ever, he decided to himself.

Miss Blair saved the two class periods after lunch for the social studies show 'n tell. "Who wants to be first?" She asked.

Willis's hand shot up. He showed the class a framed letter his great, great, great grandfather had once received from General Wade Hampton. It was about buying a hunting dog. With pride, Willis pointed to the signature.

Betty Lou had a linen dresser scarf her great, great grandmother had embroidered. It was edged with tatting. She used an unfinished piece of tatting to show the class how it was done. Johnny noticed how gracefully her hands looped the thread on her fingers, then looped the strands under and over to complete the pattern.

"A lovely piece of handwork," Miss Blair told her. "It should be preserved a long, long time."

Otis Bell displayed a small oil painting of birds at their backyard feeder. His mother had painted it.

Cecil had a newspaper clipping of himself as he stood by an uncle who wanted to be elected to the House of Representatives.

When Scott held up a pewter chess piece from a set handed down through three generations of

Jenkinses, someone said, "Aw, I thought Scott would bring his swimming pool."

Johnny laughed with the others, but it wasn't an easy laugh. He grew shakier each time a pupil sat down. Then there were no more left to volunteer.

"Johnny Elbert Finlay," called out Miss Blair.

He took a deep breath and reached into his knapsack, which he had brought from his locker at lunchtime. As he drew out the root, dirt spilled on his desk. Cecil's muffled off-key humming of "Corn Likker" could be heard along with snickering and whispering. With a stern look, Miss Blair quieted them by slapping a book down on her desk.

Now it was almost *too* quiet. Johnny paused as he stood in front of the class. A sea of wide mimicking eyes merged to make one giant monster. That monster seemed strong enough to knock Johnny off his feet. His knees felt wobbly. His insides fluttered like Aunt Lou's chickens when a red-tailed hawk came near. At that moment, he wanted to run—all the way to Mirror Mountain. There, in a quiet hollow, he'd be away from prying eyes. But it was too late. Except for the kindness in Miss Blair's voice, he might never have found courage to speak. She seemed to understand how he felt.

"This here root," Johnny said, "is ginseng. We call it 'sang' for short."

Cecil's head bobbed around as he aped Johnny's words and gestures.

Johnny bit his lip. He hadn't wanted to do this in

61

the first place, but he had no idea it would be so frightening. Please help me, he silently prayed.

Louise's face flashed across his mind's eye, and all the other eyes seemed to fade into the background. His sister was looking squarely at him, her words ringing in his ears, drowning out all the classroom noises. "Let God stand up in you, Johnny!" she seemed to be saying.

With a deep sigh, he lifted up his head and chin. He stretched himself as tall as possible. Then he put his mind on the root.

"Sang grows in rocky hollows where lots of leaves pile up," he said. "You ain't gonna find it in real soupy places, but it don't pick dry ground to grow in, neither."

In front of him, the sea of eyes became faces, and all were fixed on him. There were fewer sneers on them. He cleared his throat and went on. "Good sang diggers wait till fall when the berries ripen." He caught his breath. The quietness seemed less forced. Now, it was a quietness that was there because the kids wanted to hear what he had to tell them.

"You got to know what you're doing to dig sang roots," Johnny said with pride. "Before I dig a full growed root, I pick the berries so's I can plant 'em right where I got the root from. By next year, new sang plants'll be growing."

"How do you know when a plant's ready to dig?" Scott asked. Everyone listened intently.

"By the little bitty tail on the root," Johnny answered. "The stem grows out of that there tail every year after it shows." He held the root up to show them what he meant. "The first year, a teeny bud pops out where that stem hooks to the root. Then, this here plant had three leaves. In a year or two, it got to be a two-prong bunch. Wait two or three more years, and here's a nice root." He had pointed to the root to show them as he talked.

"Sang's good for curing what ails you. This here root is pretty old and big. I could probably sell it for ten, maybe fifteen dollars. But there ain't very many like it each year."

No one was making fun of him, now. Instead, the children were full of questions. They begged him to bring more samples of wild plants he could tell them about. This change in the way they acted toward him was more than Johnny had counted on—almost too good to be true.

"I don't know much about herbs," Miss Blair admitted when he sat down. "Lots of people don't, you know. I'd like to tell other teachers about your interesting presentation. Would you be willing to share with other classes, too?"

No one was more surprised than Johnny when he heard himself say he would. The bell rang for a short recess, and he didn't feel like running away any more.

Going home that afternoon, his eyes still sparkled with excitement as he told Sandy and Louise about his good day at school.

"I knew you had something special to share from Mirror Mountain," Sandy said, "and you were the only one who could do it."

"Aunt Lou'll help me pick the best herbs to show them other classes," Johnny said. "It's fun teaching young'uns stuff they don't know."

"Can't teach 'em if you can't read," cut in Louise.

Johnny glared at his sister. "I'm gonna get better at that too, Miss Smarty. Might even get better'n you."

Louise shot a silly grin back at him.

As they reached Mirror Mountain Road, Johnny stretched his neck toward Sandy. "C'mon, let's climb that mountain!"

A wide grin graced Sandy's profile. "We're on our way!" He almost shouted. The little bus had reached the foot of the mountain, and the motor rumbled like it had hunger in its belly. A new hunger was in Johnny, too. It had to do with going up the mountain, but more with coming back down to a friendlier world.

9
Top of the Mountain

Saturday morning, Johnny woke to the wetness of Midnight's nose on his neck.

"How'd you get in?" he chortled. Then he noticed the open window. He had slept too soundly to close it when the night cooled. "Now, just you settle down," he told the big playful dog. "We ain't goin' nowhere for a spell. Scott's coming today and we gotta wait for him."

Midnight cocked his head to one side, and whined.

"Scott's my friend from school," Johnny explained proudly.

"Johnny Elbert!" It was his mother's voice from the kitchen. "You keep that dirty-footed dog off that clean quilt; you hear?"

With a little help from Johnny, Midnight landed on the floor with a thud. Then the boy slid out of bed and pulled on his jeans and T-shirt.

After ordering Midnight to settle down on the back steps, Johnny headed for the tiny bathroom Pa had built at one end of the back porch. Aunt Lou had helped pay for the second-hand fixtures, saying "indoor plumbing is of the Lord."

When he came out of the bathroom, Johnny refused to let Midnight back in again. The dog seemed to sense that this was no ordinary Saturday, and obeyed his command to wait on the back steps.

The door to Louise's room was open. At the sound of Johnny's sneakers on the pine floor, she turned. She was wearing brown jeans and an amber T-shirt that matched her eyes. Her long hair fell forward as she bent to straighten the freshly starched ruffles of her curtains. Aunt Lou had helped her sew them from old sheets.

"Wish I had some store-bought curtains," she murmured.

"Louise, you ain't never satisfied," Johnny told her. He walked on, not waiting for a response.

"Girls worry themselves over the silliest things," he told Pa as he sat down to breakfast.

"Girls for sure ain't like boys," Pa agreed, tossing a wink Ma's way. Ma, looking pretty in a yellow flowered dress, shot him a look that was a cross between glaring and smiling. Her straight hair shone the way it always did after she'd shampooed it.

Johnny poured some honey over toasted leftover biscuits, and lit into the good breakfast.

"For a boy so squeamish about robbing bees, you sure do put away the haulings," Pa remarked.

"Just tell them bees I'm mighty obliged to 'em," Johnny replied, "but I still don't hanker to shake hands with 'em."

Pa grinned. "You got plenty of time to learn," he said. "There's a touch you have to git a'hold of to handle bees. Come's from them trustin' you and you trustin' the bees right back."

"What time your city friend gonna be here?" Ma broke in.

"About ten," Johnny answered. "I thought I'd just mosey on down to Aunt Lou's and wait out front. We'll come on up from there. I aim for me and Scott to hike up to Mirror Rock, then cross over the top to that scrubby pine grove back of them rocks."

"I ain't been there in a long time," Pa said. "Don't nobody go there."

"I know," Johnny said. "It oughta be a good place to look for arrowheads. I saw some funny-shaped rocks in them gullies one day last spring."

"I reckon it's safe enough. There ain't been much rain to wash over that slope lately. But you be careful, anyhow."

A few minutes later, Johnny waited on a stump in Aunt Lou's front yard. Sunlight poured warm from a cloudless sky. The sweet smell from sprinkles of purple basil in a nearby flower bed filled the air. Bees

67

and humming birds fanned the aroma in desperate fashion, flitting from spike to spike. It was as if they sensed that summer and its gifts would soon be gone.

Midnight's excited bark announced the arrival of a blue, four-wheel-drive van. From the driver's seat, a forty-year-old edition of Scott smiled and waved.

"Aunt Lou's bringing some lunch for us to take," Johnny announced as Scott and his father got out of the vehicle. They wore identical red striped, knitted shirts and new jeans with zippers on each pocket. Scott's new knapsack was about the same size as Johnny's.

Aunt Lou's eyes twinkled good things as she walked briskly toward them. From a basket, she put a bag lunch in each knapsack. Then she lifted out a small jar of fig preserves.

"This here's for you and Mrs. Jenkins," she said as she handed it to Scott's father.

Everyone thanked Aunt Lou. Then the boys and Midnight climbed in the back of the van for the ride to Johnny's house.

Johnny eyed his friend as they pulled into the clearing. If Scott was disappointed in the size of Johnny's home, he didn't show it. Nor did Mr. Jenkins, who smiled and moved forward to greet the other three Finlays.

Pa looked nice in freshly ironed work clothes. He had waited to meet Scott's father before going to work.

"The air feels great up here," Mr. Jenkins declared.

"It's always like that," Pa remarked.

After meeting the Finlays, Mr. Jenkins gave his son a quick goodbye hug and left, saying he'd pick him up about four that afternoon.

Pa led the way down the mountain on his dirt bike, and the boys wasted no time getting started on their hike in the other direction. Midnight bounced in and out of bushes on the way to Mirror Rock, his bark spitting out joyous warnings to all forest creatures.

Mirror Rock was a wide, flat piece of granite that could be seen from all the low country. Its gray color was what gave Mirror Mountain its name. At the place where Mirror Rock met the road, a sign read "ROAD ENDS."

"That rock is big enough to put a house on!" Scott exclaimed.

Their sneakers slapped against the granite until they found a spot where they could look down at Cougarville. The air was clear; the sun, toasty warm.

"See them long squashed-down buildings to the right?" Johnny pointed. "That's Cougarville Textiles."

Scott's brown eyes sparkled with excitement. "Hey, look—I can cover the whole mill with one hand!" From his knapsack, he brought out a pair of binoculars. After a quick look, he passed them to Johnny.

It was a new experience for Johnny. Everything he had seen at a distance looked closer to him when viewed through the binoculars. Scott pointed out his house, a big stone one. It was surrounded by green lawns and clumps of trees.

"That little circle of blue is our swimming pool,"

Scott said. "We'll swim in it when you come visit."

Johnny forced a straight face, so the happy excitement inside him wouldn't make him look silly.

"Don't go past that crack in the rock," he cautioned Scott, who was moving near the edge. "Just follow me. I know a good place you can see down from."

A few feet from where they had been, he led his friend to a slightly lower ridge. For protection, a wire rope was stretched across the outer edge.

"Almost makes me dizzy to look down so far," Scott said. Suddenly, he gasped. "There's a truck down there!" He cried.

Johnny shrugged. "Been down there for years," he said. "Some dummy parked it on the rock and went hiking. When he come back, it'd rolled right over the edge. To this day, ain't nobody ever figured how to get it outta them rocks."

"Wow!" Scott shook his head.

They took the path that crossed the top of Mirror Mountain. It was called Top Trail.

"Why aren't there more trees up here?" Scott asked.

"They're dying out. Pa says it weren't always that way. He said they was green as green could be when he was a boy my size. Now them big trees just keep a'dying. Little ones try to come along. But they don't grow very tall before they droop over like they're gonna vomit."

"That's terrible. What's causing it?"

"Pa thinks it's the pollution from cars and factories. He says it must be drifting in the high air."

"I'll ask my dad," Scott declared. "I know he wouldn't want smoke from his mill to do something like this."

A rustling sound from below them caused the boys to whirl around. It was only Midnight, leaping and loping through the underbrush. But something else caught Johnny's eye. Followed by Scott, he scrambled down the slope to a circle of small trees about as high as his waist. A tall plastic pop bottle was tied upside down to the trunk of each one. The bottle's neck was buried in the soil, and its bottom had been sliced out so water could be poured in it.

"Hmmmm —," Johnny mused, "I reckon Hank and Rusty wasn't storying about watering trees up here."

"Who's Hank and Rusty?"

Johnny shared his doubts about the two young men, and his plans for them to check out their cabin.

Scott was excited over the idea of spying on the place, but was beginning to get tired. Sweat stood in little beads on his tanned forehead. "How far is it?" He asked.

"Nigh onto a mile by the high path," Johnny answered, "but we'll take a short cut."

He led his friend along the ravine until they came to a big sycamore. Dark, ghostly leaf shadows danced on its pale gray trunk, but a bright gleam of mischief stood in Johnny's eye. He pointed to a wide thicket of mountain laurel. Like a giant green comforter, it spread across the sloping mountainside. Beyond, amid rocks and trees, snatches of Way High Creek sparkled in the sunlight.

71

"That looks like a pretty dense thicket; isn't it?" asked Scott. "I don't see a path. How are we goin' to get through it?"

Johnny grinned. "That's the fun thing," he said, "we ain't goin' through 'em. We gonna squirrel across!"

"Squirrel?" Scott's eyes were two big question marks.

"Don't fret yourself; just follow me." Taking hold of the top branch of a laurel bush, Johnny lifted his limber form quickly to the next one.

Scott let out a shout of approval, and followed. Amid whoops of glee, the boys flitted from branch to branch without touching the ground. Midnight's head bobbed in and out of the thick leaves beneath them; his excited bark cheered them on.

Scott lost his grip once, and disappeared in the soft cushion of leaves. Soon, his head popped up again. Laughing, he pulled himself up and swung along behind Johnny.

Soon the boys could hear Way High Creek swishing over rocks. Beyond the creek, the sound of motorcyles heading down the mountain road went from loud to steady; then faded.

"Just in time," Johnny announced. "They done made it halfway down the mountain." He was pleased that, thus far, his plan was going well.

10
More than Arrowheads

The boys walked the big log to cross the creek. A little shiver went over Johnny as he remembered his meeting with Corn Kelly two days before.

The feeling was short-lived. There was nothing dreary about the area today. Little fingers of bright sunlight reached through the trees and warmed their shoulders.

The cabin was a wide log house. The huge stone chimneys at each end were exactly alike. A tall gable, framed by rustic logs, centered the roof.

"Pa says he don't know why Uncle Elbert stuck that

gable up there," Johnny said as he noticed Scott looking up at it.

"Makes it look like a little church," Scott observed.

Johnny peered at the building with narrowed eyes. "Don't it, though? I never noticed that before."

Shades were drawn on the front windows. Johnny went on the porch and knocked. "Nope," he said in a pleased voice, "ain't nobody home."

Midnight sniffed about the yard as the boys went to the back. There, they found a small patch of turnip greens growing, but nothing else.

Near the fireplace on the east wall they peeped through a wide window door. From that point, they could see almost the whole large room.

Johnny recognized some of the furniture. Uncle Elbert's old couch was still there. Beside it, papers and large books were stacked on the floor. He didn't remember a slanted table to which a drawing lamp was attached. Papers that looked like sketches were clamped to the table. Beyond it, in the dim light beneath the shaded windows, the floor was dotted with small groups of leaves, berries and cones. Each pile had a white tag on top.

The boys cupped their hands over their eyes to see better. To Johnny, none of the stacks looked like roots or herbs he might value.

They tried the door; it was locked.

"Are we going to try the windows?" Scott wanted to know.

"I reckon not. Pa wouldn't want me to break into

74

nobody's house, not even Aunt Lou's." He checked the windows anyhow, and found them locked.

Two curtained bedrooms jutted out beside the window door. There was a bathroom between them, Johnny remembered. At the west end of the building a few dirty dishes were piled in the kitchen sink.

"There just ain't any complete answers at this here cabin," Johnny decided. "We'd best move on."

Through woods graced with silverbell, poplar and oaks, the boys and the big black dog tromped. Soon the big rocks which hid the pine grove from view were in front of them.

They scrambled over and around the rocks. Midnight whimpered in protest as he was forced to squeeze through small crevices beneath the rocks to follow.

Scott found an arrowhead in a gully. "It looks like a Morrow Mountain Projectile Point!" he exclaimed with several twists of his mouth that amazed Johnny.

"This here's *Mirror* Mountain," Johnny corrected.

Scott laughed. He explained that "Morrow Mountain" was a name classification of Indian weaponheads. "You go by the shape," he added. "This could be 6,000 years old." His brown eyes were bright with excitement.

"You sure know lots about 'em," Johnny marvelled.

"Not really," Scott replied. "I just read a lot. If you want, I'll loan you one of my books."

"Maybe later," Johnny answered. "I-I don't read so good yet." He shifted his glance from Scott to scan the pine-dotted slope. The trees were scrawny, clad scantily with needles. The grove covered a good 2,000 yards of the steep, downward slope.

"Hand me your binoculars a minute," Johnny said. "I want to get a better look at them tall, green plants. I've never seen anything like that growin' under them pines before."

He peered through the binoculars, then gave them back to Scott. "Let's go see 'em up close," he said.

"Pop bottles again!" Scott exclaimed as they stood by one of the plants.

"Ummmm-hummh. Somebody's been doing a powerful lot of gardening on this here mountain. You know what marijuana looks like?"

Scott shook his head, his eyes widening. "Do you think that's what this is?"

"I don't know. I never saw it for real—just pictures on TV." Johnny picked a few leaves and pushed them to the bottom of his knapsack. "I'll ask Aunt Lou. If it ain't a mountain plant, she'll know."

"Do you think Hank and Rusty planted them?"

"Looks that way. Reckon they could've found this here place and toted water here, too. But for sure, these ain't no little mountain trees."

He looked in every direction. The lower end of the slope overhung the road that went to the other side of the mountain. Rocks jutted over the edge of that road. It would be very difficult for anyone to enter the grove from that side. But a jagged path might be carved, if someone had a mind to do so.

Johnny looked at Scott. Mr. Jenkins had trusted him to keep the younger boy safe. He sensed danger in the pine grove. If the plants were marijuana, the person who planted them was breaking the law, and he sure wouldn't want any boys snooping around. It could mean trouble.

"It's time for us to eat," Johnny said, trying to keep his voice steady. "We'd best be going."

Near the creek, they reached a shady glade where a spring bubbled out of the rocky hillside. A small gully carried its overflow to the creek.

"This is the best fried chicken I ever tasted!" Scott's cheeks glistened with juice from the tender drumstick. Midnight sat close by and eyed him intently. Scott gave in to the pleading look in the dog's eyes and left a little of the meat on the bone. Midnight caught it in mid-air when he tossed it to him. Scott could afford to share his lunch. Aunt Lou had packed more than enough for the two boys.

"Everything Aunt Lou fixes is good," Johnny agreed. He finished off a deviled egg, then scooped up a handful of spring water. When Scott finished eating, he cupped his hands the way Johnny did for a drink.

"Best water I've ever tasted," Scott declared.

After lunch, they found two empty cans and rolled up the legs of their jeans. In the clear sunlit water on the edge of the creek, they dipped up minnows for bait. Johnny brought out a small tin box from his pocket. In it were hooks, lead, cork, and a small roll of fishline.

They caught shiny little sunfish, which they tossed back. Time flew as they watched the corks bob in the current.

"You're so lucky to live on this mountain," Scott said. "I could stay on and on and never get bored."

"Yup," Johnny agreed, "but it's nigh on to 3:30. We'd best get back to my house."

Scott glanced at his watch. "Hey, it *is* 3:30," he said, surprised. "How'd you know without a watch?"

"By sun and shadows," Johnny replied. "Mountain folks don't need time pieces. You got a nice watch, though."

When they reached Johnny's house, the Jenkinses were already there. Scott's mother and sister had come, too. Louise and Donna sat and talked on the big rock while Mrs. Jenkins admired Ma's willow baskets and cornshuck mats.

Ma smiled at Johnny. "Your Pa done carted off Mr. Jenkins to see them beegums out back," she told him.

"What's beegums?" Scott asked, and Johnny explained they were bee hives made from the trunks of gum trees.

Mrs. Jenkins bought a number of Ma's baskets and foot mats for gifts. She invited Louise and Johnny to visit at the Jenkins home soon. When they left, Pa insisted that a quart of his sourwood honey should go with them. It was a gift from the Finlays to the Jenkinses, he said.

That night, after they were in their beds, Johnny and Louise talked. Louise pushed back the quilt that

78

covered her side of the thin partition. This way, they could hear each other.

"There's that Donna," Louise said. "She's bound to have the prettiest room a girl could want, and full of pretty things. Yet she said my quilt was just beautiful."

"And Scott acts like we got the best there is right here on the mountain," Johnny put in between yawns.

"Them Jenkinses put me to mind of Sandy McRee," Louise went on. "They make you feel like they see God a-standing tall in you, don't they, Johnny?"

No answer came through the thin partition. Johnny had drifted off to sleep. It was the peaceful kind that always followed a carefree day on the mountain.

11
Church on the Mountain

It had been a bright day the previous spring when Sandy McRee had first hiked up Mirror Mountain and introduced himself to the Finlays. He was amazed to find that people on the mountain had to drive to Cougarville for church. Most of them didn't have good cars to take them, so most of them didn't go.

With the help of Aunt Lou and some others, Sandy had started a small church group on her front porch. Soon the number grew to thirty, forty; then fifty. A larger meeting place was needed, so Pa and some of the men helped Sandy build an old-time brush arbor.

It sat near a little spring across the road from Aunt Lou's. That way, the worshippers could use her bathroom.

Except for his cousins, Ray Arthur and Cindy, Johnny couldn't remember when other children had lived on the mountain. Most of the families had moved to Cougarville when Johnny was a baby. But they came back to what they called their "Church on the Mountain" as soon as they learned of the chance to gather with old friends on the mountain.

Services started at eleven; hugging and talking started much earlier. Most members brought lunch in coolers for a picnic after church.

At ten thirty sharp, Pa strapped on his guitar. Someone yelled, "Hit it, Earle!" George Turner's fiddle bow waved up and down, while Lonnie Shook's fingers slid across his banjo's frets like lightning. Anyone who brought an instrument could join in, and anyone who wanted to sing a solo could do so.

Mrs. Ethel Carver always sang four or five long verses of the most mournful hymn possible — or so it seemed to Johnny. He was always glad for her to finish so Pa could lead out in perky songs that bounced merrily off the mountainside toward heaven. Hands clapped and toes tapped when they sang, "I Saw the Light."

Fast picking and loud singing were still going on when Sandy arrived just before eleven.

But today he wasn't alone. With him was none other than Miss Blair! Soft "oohs" and "ahhs" drifted through the congregation when Sandy introduced her as "my friend." She wore a blue dress that matched her eyes. She smiled and nodded at the crowd, then sat down.

Sandy took his place at the altar that had been built with treated timber from Doug Warren's sawmill. A swarm of "amens" swept over the arbor when Sandy reminded everyone that bad weather hadn't spoiled a single service all summer. But, he went on, cold weather would soon make outdoor services unwise. Uncle Elbert was selected as the head of a committee to study the problem.

At prayer time, everyone prayed aloud at the same time. They prayed for the sick, for rain, and for a church building.

Miss Lizzie West, who took up two places on a bench, got excited. For a minute or two, her high-pitched voice rose over the others. Then she grew quiet, and finally, only Sandy prayed.

Cindy was thirteen, with laughing blue-green eyes and curls the color of copper. Ray Arthur was a red-headed, freckle-faced twelve. The cousins were allowed to sit together as long as they behaved. That meant no whispering, fly catching, bumblebee swatting, and especially no giggling, which was hardest. The four cousins sat on a bench at the back.

Sandy was well into the sermon when Johnny saw a pale face duck in back of a bush near the spring. It was Maybelle Kelly, Corn's shy little wife. Aunt Lou had said Corn wouldn't hear of her coming to church. Well, he had news for Aunt Lou. Maybelle was just sneaking up and listening, anyhow.

He turned to see if Ray Arthur had noticed May-belle, too. He hadn't. His cousin's mischievous glance was fixed on a chameleon that had slithered up the back of Miss Lizzie's yellow dress. The tiny creature had turned as yellow as the dress itself. Ray Arthur shook with silent laughter. Johnny put his hand over his mouth and clenched his teeth good and hard. When the tiny chameleon reached the woman's fat neck, she jumped up and swatted it off with a loud shriek. Someone near her stomped the poor, tiny creature. Both boys spit out giggles with gurgling sounds their hands weren't able to muffle.

Within seconds, they were painfully aware of their shoulders being firmly grasped. For the rest of the service, their mothers sat betweem them. There was nothing else to do, and they listened to Sandy's sermon.

The picnic broke up earlier than usual that day because smoky rain clouds were gathering.

"Praise the Lord for the rain that's a-coming!" the people shouted. They hugged each other all over again and started home.

Sandy and Miss Blair were invited to "set a spell" with all the Finlays at Aunt Lou's. Sandy thanked her for the invitation, but said he'd promised to show "Jenny" the view from Mirror Rock. They drove off in that direction.

Immediately, the idea came to Ray Arthur that he and Johnny should sneak up the rock and eavesdrop.

"Don't let Midnight out of the barn yet," he told Johnny.

To keep the dog quiet, Johnny sneaked some table scraps to him. Midnight was always locked up for the duration of the picnic.

The boys hurried through the woods to Mirror Rock. They crept up quietly and hid behind a clump of bushes.

The couple viewed the countryside from the rock. Wisps of moist air lifted Jenny Blair's soft brown curls. Sandy couldn't seem to take his eyes off her pretty face.

"I was pleased that Johnny did so well on that social studies assignment," she said. "Your people up here are wonderful, Sandy."

"You're quite a wonder, yourself." Sandy's voice was soft, shaky.

"I'd love to come back again—if you think I could help."

"Could you ever! Aunt Lou's been praying for a good Sunday school teacher. She'd say it was 'of the Lord' that you came along." His hand closed over hers. "I say so, too."

Back in the bushes, Ray Arthur whispered, "Any minute now, he's gonna kiss her!"

"If he does, I'll throw up," Johnny murmured. His mouth curled down to feign nausea.

With no warning at all, a mighty clap of lightning bounced off the mountain nearby, and rain began to fall.

The boys didn't even wait to see Sandy and Miss Blair rush to the yellow station wagon and start down the mountain. Instead, they tore through the woods to Johnny's house. There, they built a fire in the fireplace to dry their wet clothes before their parents arrived. But Uncle Elbert was in a hurry to leave before the clothes were ready, and Ray Arthur had to wear an old pair of Pa's coveralls home.

12
Trouble

Monday morning, Johnny overslept. He was roused by Louise, who shook him until he sat up.

"Ma ain't feeling good," she told him. "Pa went to borrow Uncle Elbert's car to take her to the doctor."

There wasn't time to eat breakfast. Johnny dressed in a hurry. Still half asleep, he stuffed his books in the knapsack and rushed out to the waiting school bus.

Midnight jumped up and jostled him. Before getting on the bus, he patted the dog's head. Early morning outings with Midnight just didn't happen very often any more.

As Johnny sat beside Louise, a stirred-up tightness crept from his stomach to his throat. Ma often felt poorly, but she never seemed to need a doctor.

"Is Ma bad off?" He asked his sister.

There was a worried look in Louise's amber eyes. Her cheeks were pale, as if she'd forgotten to put on the tiny bit of makeup Ma let her use.

"Just because a person needs to see a doctor doesn't mean there's anything to be afraid of," Sandy put in from the driver's seat. "Usually the doctor can take care of it with no problem."

Johnny's face darkened. "That's not the way it was with Aunt Sophie. She was Ma's sister, and she got bad sick. When they got her to the doctor, it was too late. She died."

"Hey now," Sandy admonished, "you're counting chickens before they hatch. Why worry when we can pray? Are you with me?"

It seemed so easy, the way Sandy talked to God. He just kept his eyes on the road and prayed aloud while he steered and braked the bus down the mountain.

Johnny felt better. It amazed him how God didn't get to sit down for a minute in Sandy McRee. God stood, walked, and travelled in the sturdy young man.

When they reached the schoolyard, Louise blotted her wet cheeks with a kleenex, but there was a glow about her quiet smile. Funny, thought Johnny, how girls cried and smiled all at the same time.

It was recess before Johnny and Scott had a chance to talk.

"What did your Aunt Lou say about the leaves?" Scott asked in a low voice.

Johnny's mouth flew open. "I plumb forgot to ask her! Them leaves are still in my knapsack. But it's locked up in my locker. I'll stop by Aunt Lou's on the way home, for sure."

Scott's eyes were wide and anxious. "Better be careful. If they're really marijuana, it's against the law to have them."

"Don't worry," Johnny assured him, "I ain't gonna disturb them weeds till I see the whites of Aunt Lou's eyes!"

The day seemed to be shaping up to be a good one. Johnny did so well in reading, Miss Blair praised him before the class.

"Johnny missed a lot of school," she reminded them, "but he's working hard to catch up, and I'm sure he will." She sounded like Sandy talking; positive, good things would happen. All day long, he worked to make her proud of him.

The last period of the day was free for homework. Johnny had almost finished his arithmetic when the principal's voice came blaring from the intercom: "Please send Johnny Elbert Finlay to my office right away."

To hear his name coming out of the box was enough in itself to frighten him. Miss Blair's puzzled nod didn't help. What could it be about? He felt his heart pounding as he opened the door to Mr. Coleman's office.

The stocky-built principal sat at his desk by a window that overlooked the schoolyard. Several times the jolly black man had spoken to Johnny in the hall. Not only was he liked by the children; they respected him. They knew that, although Mr. Coleman joked a lot, he could be firm when he needed to be.

Next to Mr. Coleman stood a tall young man with deep-set gray eyes that seemed to slice Johnny into chips at first glance. On a leash beside the officer, a big German shepherd sat in a relaxed position. With all three sets of eyes fixed on him, Johnny felt a cold chill race through his body.

"Johnny, this is Sgt. Cartwright," Mr. Coleman said. "His dog, Pal, is especially trained to find things with his nose."

Johnny's face wrinkled up in a puzzled frown.

With a long, muscular arm, Sgt. Cartwright reached behind the desk and drew something up. "Recognize this?" he asked, as he plopped Johnny's knapsack on the desk.

Johnny swallowed to dislodge the hard knot in his throat, then nodded. Now, he knew why Scott had seemed so anxious at recess.

The officer turned the knapsack upside down. The green leaves, now wilted, fell on Mr. Coleman's desk with a sick plop, and Johnny knew he had correctly guessed their identity from the start.

The two men waited in silence, their eyes never veering from Johnny's face. For a long moment, words would not come. Why, he thought, hadn't he remembered to remove the leaves before leaving for school this morning?

"Did you hear Sgt. Cartwright?" Mr. Coleman asked.

"Where did you get those leaves."

"I-I picked them off a bush," Johnny heard himself say.

"What kind of bush?"

He cleared his throat. It was a dry cough. He had no hope that his mouth would find the right words to say now, but he went on. "I don't rightly know," he answered. "I was gonna ask my Aunt Lou. She knows every plant on the mountain. I never saw one like this up there before."

A heavy silence fell. In it, the two men looked at each other in a strange way. Mr. Coleman's dark eyes were serious as he drummed his plump fingers on the desk. The bell rang, but no one moved to dismiss him.

Johnny told them how he had found the patch of plants in the pine grove. He didn't mention Scott's being with him. This was his own trouble. He couldn't let his friend be involved—not even if Scott might no longer be his friend. Bad news travelled fast. The Jenkinses would hear, and say "no more!"

"Who do you think planted it?" Mr. Coleman asked.

Johnny shook his head. He thought about Hank and Rusty.

"What's your father doing these days?" Sgt. Cartwright asked.

Johnny sucked in a big gulp of air as his wide face reddened with anger. "Working at my Uncle Elbert's store . . . every day!" he stated. "My Pa ain't been doing nothing that ain't legal!"

"Now, Johnny," Mr. Coleman drawled in a kind voice.

91

"We're not saying that he has."

"But you're getting ready to, and it ain't so."

Then Sgt. Cartwright explained how Pal had been brought to sniff out marijuana in the school lockers, and had led them to Johnny's knapsack.

"You may know more than you've told us, Johnny," the officer added, "but I'm inclined to think you're telling the truth. If you are, I know you'll help us by not telling anyone about this. Can you promise that?"

The noisy chatter and stomping feet of children in the halls was fading. Sandy would be waiting outside. If he waited any longer, there would be questions he must not answer yet. "Y-yessir," Johnny said. "You can be sure of it."

Mr. Coleman gave Johnny his empty knapsack and dismissed him. When he returned to the classroom, it was empty. Relieved to find it that way, he threw his books in the knapsack and hurried out.

13
A Restless Night

As Johnny rode home, troubled thoughts buzzed in his head like bees in a flowering sourwood tree. Little knots in his stomach seemed to tighten and grow into a ball that would never come undone again.

Johnny was sure the officer hadn't believed him when he said Pa had nothing to do with the marijuana patch. Whatever Sgt. Cartwright had said, he suspected Pa. Now Johnny was sorry he'd promised not to tell anyone. Pa'd be the first to say "a man's word ought to be his bond." He'd heard Pa say that lots of times.

Maybe he should go ahead and warn his father, anyhow. Sandy had said God didn't just forgive the bad things a person did before becoming a Christian; He also forgot about them, as if they had never happened. If only people were like that. Johnny was sure Mr. Coleman and Sgt. Cartwright knew about Pa's record for moonshinin'. Guilty or not, Pa'd be the first one accused of growing the marijuana.

"Johnny, you haven't said one word all the way up the mountain," Sandy said as the bus reached the clearing.

Johnny shrugged his shoulders. A choppy, whirring sound filled the air above them when Sandy cut off the ignition.

"It's a helicopter!" Louise nudged Johnny to get out so she could see the chopper.

Sandy got out to meet Pa, who was coming their way. Johnny noticed his father had on his good dark pants and a white shirt, then remembered Ma being sick and going to the doctor. With all the trouble he'd had, his worry about her had been pushed into a little corner of his mind.

Pa's hazel eyes squinted up at the chopper. It dipped down and up, flattening treetops as it hovered over them.

"That there's a sheriff's chopper," Pa observed. "Sure glad I ain't got no stills to be found."

"Pa, I need to talk to you." Johnny drew in a shaky breath.

"How's Ma?" Louise butted in, her voice tense and anxious. She was worried about Ma.

Pa's pug nose spread out as he smiled. "She's feeling better and insisting on cooking supper," he said.

"Doc gave her some medicine. Gonna put her in the hospital next week. Doc says a little operation'll fix 'er up just fine. Says there ain't nothing to worry about."

"But operations and hospitals cost lots of money," Louise worried.

Pa nodded. "I know. Reckon the Lord's looking after us real good. Two months back, Elbert took out insurance on his workers and their families. It's gonna take care of the cost."

"Does she have cancer?" Johnny's eyes were troubled.

"Doc says, rest assured it ain't."

Sandy touched Johnny's shoulder. "You see? God's the real healer we can count on."

"Sure is," Pa agreed. "Things look brighter and shinier every day!"

"So get that worried look off your face," Sandy told Johnny. "Your Ma will be just *fine*!"

Johnny nodded and forced a little smile as Sandy got in the station wagon and drove away.

Even if Pa had heard Johnny ask to talk to him, he'd forgotten. Just as well, thought Johnny. With everyone so happy over Ma not being bad off sick, he couldn't spoil it for them. Not now, anyhow. The jovial mood would end soon enough. When the marijuana patch was sighted, people would be questioned. Pa was known to be the best moonshiner on the mountain. Now that he didn't make moonshine any more, they'd figure he would be just as good at growing marijuana. Ma would cry, and Pa's face would fill up with gloom. Just when school was getting bearable, Johnny would have to face loneliness and sneers all over again.

After supper, Johnny said he had homework to do. As he closed the door to his room, he heard Ma wonder if he was sick. "Hardly touched his supper," she said.

"He's just getting to that moody age," Pa told her. "He'll snap out of it. Best leave him be."

When he had a tiff with Louise, Johnny welcomed being left to himself. Tonight, however, there was nothing peaceful about being alone. His thoughts whirled around in little circles in his head. He didn't try to study.

Finally, he slept. In a dream, he was again at school, where everyone laughed and pointed at him. Cecil Harwood's voice boomed from the intercom: "Johnny Elbert Finlay's father was busted for growing marijuana on Mirror Mountain. Now, that's a real special something to come from his precious mountain. Don't you all agree?"

Miss Blair's blue eyes were no longer soft and understanding. In a voice that didn't sound like her own at all, she ordered Johnny to sit in a chair that faced the wall. Then she clapped hands with the children as they sang, "Corn Likker."

14
Stalking the Quarry

The taunting sound of "Corn Likker" rang in Johnny's ears. He cupped his hands on them and the words went together and became "Click-A!"

He blinked his eyes against the glare of the single light bulb being switched on above him.

"Wake up, Johnny Elbert!" It was Louise, calling him in a quiet voice. "You was sobbing something awful," his sister said.

"I was dreaming something awful," he told her. "What time is it?"

"Still too early for Ma and Pa to be up—much less me and you."

Johnny's small form jerked as he tried to hold back

tears, but Louise knew it was more than just a bad dream that troubled him.

"You want to talk about whatever it is?" she asked.

Before he even thought about it, Johnny had told her everything he had held inside. He started with the discovery of the plants in the pine grove, then the trouble it caused him at school. He wound up his story with the helicopter they had seen hovering over the mountain.

"You sure did open up a big old can of worms when you went to that pine grove," Louise agreed.

"I'm so scared, Louise," Johnny blurted out. "They think Pa planted that stuff. Do you think . . . ?"

"Thinking ain't knowing," Louise clipped. "Get your clothes on while I do the same. Before they try to pin this on our Pa, you and me are gonna find out just who did plant them weeds on our mountain."

"All right!" Johnny exclaimed.

"Shhh! Listen," Louise cautioned. The only sound they could hear was the rhythmic murmur of Pa's snoring.

"I don't reckon nobody'll hear us over that," Louise snickered.

A few minutes later, the two children eased out of Johnny's window. He could hardly believe Louise was on his side, helping him. At the same time, he felt as if a load had been lifted from his shoulders.

Outside, it was chilly. Louise tied a kerchief about her long hair. She said she was glad they had on long-sleeved T-shirts under their windbreakers.

"You know the best way to get up there, Johnny. I'll follow."

In semi-darkness, they hurried up the road toward Mirror Rock.

The smell of wet woods rose to greet them as, a few minutes later, they whipped along the trail across the mountaintop.

At gray dawn, they reached the rocks that hid the pine grove, and stopped.

"We'll have to hide where we can see over them rocks," Johnny said.

He chose a full-grown sweetgum with strong, upstretched limbs. Its thick covering of leaves was a scramble of fading green, gold and crimson, not quite ready to become part of the forest floor.

He ran his hands over the moist trunk of the tree and turned to Louise. "Maybe you'd better hide over there back of one of them rocks," he suggested.

Louise glared sternly at her brother. "I got my jeans on, and I can still climb higher'n any boy," she declared in a stubborn, proud voice. "Fact is, I'm going first. Time's a-wasting."

Holding back his annoyance, he stepped aside and let her go up ahead of him. They climbed from limb to limb until Louise decided they were high enough for viewing the area beyond the rocks. With heels pressed to the tree trunk, they rested on their stomachs and waited.

Waking-up noises of forest creatures were all around them.

"This here tree climbing puts me to mind of when we was littler," Louise said.

That was before Louise started trying to act grown-up, thought Johnny. She'd been such a tomboy, then—more fun. A quiet feeling slipped into him. His sister could be so bossy and critical, but he knew she loved him, and he loved her, too. Especially right now.

"I feel better on this mountain than anywhere," he said in a hushed voice. "I been thinking I might not go back to school—not ever."

"You know you ain't gonna be able to do nothing worth much if you don't," Louise said in an even voice.

"But its such a drag. Like yesterday, I was doing good." He took a deep breath and let it out in a little sigh. "Miss Blair said I could read as good as anybody. The young'uns was friendly. It seemed right for me to be there. Then the law came and changed it all back."

"It still ain't easy for me," Louise admitted. "I been doing my best to catch up. Sometimes I cry. But I just ain't gonna give up."

"Well, just s'pose it turns out Pa's the one who planted that weed out there. You still gonna go back and have them staring and pointing fingers at you?"

She sighed. "Shame on you for thinking such a thing. You know Pa didn't do it. But even if he did, I'd still go back to school. I wouldn't want to, but no matter how hurtful it is, I got to get educated. Anyhow, you know nary one of us got a choice. It's the law."

"Down there ain't like up here on the mountain,"

Johnny mused. "Up here, everything pulls together like some great, big hands was in it—rocks and dirt; wet times, dry times."

"That's God's hands you're talking about. He put all them little animals, birds and insects down and said, 'Live!' They don't put up no argument. They just do like they're told to do. You and me ain't got no right to live halfway, neither."

He took a deep breath. "Reckon not. Sometimes I wish I was one of them little critters that ain't suppose to leave the mountain. But I guess I'm not. No matter how much I hate to, I got to go to school."

"Shhh!" Louise warned. "Someone's coming."

Johnny could hear men's voices coming from the direction of Mirror Rock. Both children remained stark still, listening.

Two men in camouflage fatigues approached the tall rocks. Johnny peeped through the leaves. The men picked out a crevice in the high rocks, which gave them a view of the pine grove.

"Lawmen!" he whispered to Louise.

The men were too close. Johnny and Louise dared not move, lest their presence be discovered.

"I'll circle around and lie in that tall grass near the bottom of the slope," one man said in a hushed voice. He was a short man. His cap matched his fatigues that were too big for him. The children watched him creep through the grove and stretch himself on his stomach in a clump of high weeds.

The other man was chunky-built, with a little gray

101

moustache that tilted upward on each end.

On the ground under the tree, a pair of doves and some sparrows foraged for worms. A crisp wind now bounced off the rocks, and there was a whisper of leaves falling from nearby trees. Johnny hoped the sounds would drown out others that might give away their hideout.

Suddenly, the birds splashed upward as a jet black streak bounded from the woods. Midnight had trailed them perfectly.

The dog sat beneath the tree, looked up and scolded the children with high-pitched moans. Johnny met Louise's helpless glance. He clenched his teeth as he saw the man in the rocks watching Midnight. Then the man said something in his walkie-talkie, and crept quietly toward the tree, one hand in his jacket. Johnny was sure he had a gun there. The two children cast frightened glances at each other. Midnight was churning up a growl, and Johnny felt as if his breath was cut off.

In the distance, they could hear their school bus making its daily climb up the mountain. At that moment, Johnny wished he was on it.

"What are you kids doing up there?" The man's voice was stern and hard. "Come down and get this hound away from here!" Midnight's growl was getting louder.

"Y-yessir," Johnny said. He moved to start climbing down as he snapped "Quiet, Midnight!" as softly as he could.

Through the spaces between the fluttering leaves,

the children saw the figure of a man enter the grove from the lower end that overhung the road. The man was big, with a beard, and carried a bucket. That figured. Sunday's rain hadn't been enough, though it had poured hard on the boys as they ran home from Mirror Rock. If only he had Scott's binoculars now, thought Johnny.

The bearded man moved up the slope. One by one, he bent over each plant, as if to check it. Once or twice, he added water to the plastic pop bottle attached to a plant. Except for muffled whines, Midnight remained still and quiet, his eyes on Johnny.

With startling quickness, the man in the tall weeds popped up from his hiding place. His gruff "Freeze!" bounced off the rocks and echoed down the mountainside.

"Don't shoot—*please* don't shoot!" pleaded the bearded man in a raspy voice, hands over his head. "I ain't gonna give you no trouble."

In a wonderful sigh of relief, Johnny let out the breath he had been holding. He scrambled out of the tree, with Louise right behind him.

On the ground, Louise threw her arms around her brother, and gave him a bear hug. Tears ran down her cheeks. "It ain't Pa! It ain't Pa!" she squealed in his ear.

"I *know*!" Johnny shouted. "It's Corn Kelly!"

15
Celebrities

As soon as the lawmen had fastened handcuffs on Corn, they escorted him to the trail that led across the top of the mountain to Mirror Rock where their truck was parked.

The children dashed home the shortest way they knew. At the edge of the clearing, they met Pa coming to look for them. His short face was flushed, his pug nose taut, and his thin-lipped mouth curved downward.

"Where've you young'uns been?" he roared. "Your Ma's all worried up about you, and I'm late for work, not to mention Sandy making that trip up and down the mountain for nothin'!" His nostrils flared with fury. "I oughta tan both your hides!"

"Pa, please just hear what happened," Johnny pleaded.

Their father took a deep breath and let it out with a shudder. "Might as well," he said in a quieter tone. "Come on to the house so Ma can hear, too. But it better be good!"

Both parents listened carefully as Johnny poured out his story. He told how the marijuana-sniffing police dog found the leaves in his knapsack; of his fear that the lawmen would be after Pa again. When he got to that point, all of the frustration and loneliness of the past twenty-four hours seemed to surface.

Pa's eyes were moist as he put his arms around his son and hugged him tight. Johnny sobbed with the wonderful relief that was only to be found by leaning on his father.

Then it was Louise's turn to talk. She finished the story at the moment they heard the lawmen's truck pass the clearing on its way down the mountain. Corn Kelly wouldn't be around to frighten him for awhile, Johnny thought with relief.

Ma got up and started opening cabinets and packing food in a basket. At first Pa didn't seem to notice.

"I knowed someone could climb that bank from the road if they had a mind to," Johnny said, wiping his eyes on his sleeve. "I just didn't think about it being Corn."

"He'd be the most likely one," Louise said knowingly. "Without Pa to help, he couldn't make no decent corn likker, for sure."

"Well, it is a mite unnerving," Pa mused. "If it weren't for having the Lord's concerns in me, that could be me handcuffed in that there truck going down the mountain."

"Praise the Lord that it ain't," Ma put in. "Right now, you better get yourself on that little dirt bike and ride; elsewise, Elbert's gonna lose his concerns for *you*!" She set the basket on the table in front of him.

"What's that food for?" Pa rose and grabbed his helmet from the hook by the door.

"First off, it's for you to leave at Aunt Lou's. Tell her me and Midnight's a-walking back of you."

Louise frowned. "Aunt Lou don't need no food."

"Ain't for her. That poor little wife of Corn's gonna need all the looking after we can give till her folks can come for her," Ma explained. "You young'uns make yourselves some peanut butter sandwiches and rest a spell. Me and Aunt Lou's gonna walk over to see Maybelle." No one had the slightest doubt that Aunt Lou would do exactly as Ma expected.

Pa's eyes were shining with a mischievous look as he put on his riding helmet. "Sure I can't give you a lift, Mae Beth?" He said to Ma.

She grinned. "Get goin', man!" she ordered with a wave of her long arms. "You know I ain't getting on that crazy bike."

Midnight eyed the children as they laid out the makings of their sandwiches.

"You go to Aunt Lou-ooooh!" Johnny ordered. After one pleading look, Midnight accepted that his friend was serious, and the dog followed Ma out.

Forgetting about resting, Johnny and Louise gulped down their snack and hurried back to the pine grove. They walked around the marijuana patch to the little cliff above the old road. There from a gnarled old oak that hung out over the steep drop was a rope running through a pulley attached to a limb of the tree.

"Look at that," said Louise. "That must be how Corn pulled buckets of water up here to water his plants."

"Yeah, but you know what I'm thinkin'? I'm fixin' to make a swing out of it," said Johnny.

"You'd kill yourself from up here," protested Louise.

"No I wouldn't."

Just then they heard the motor of a truck grinding away as it crawled up the rugged old road. It was a state truck painted orange with a work crew riding in the back. The big dump truck parked right below Johnny and Louise, and the men climbed up the narrow path to the marijuana patch.

Johnny and Louise watched as the men pulled the plants up by their roots and threw them off the clifff into the back of the truck. The men worked fast, and soon all the large plants were gone. Then, using hoes, they began chopping all the small shoots.

Just then another helicopter buzzed in over the trees and began circling the area. This one, however, was painted blue with "Channel 2-TV" in huge, red and white letters on the side. Johnny and Louise could see a cameraman taking aerial pictures from the open side door. The chopper circled several times, then seemed to hop right over the top of Mirror Mountain. The kids could hear its sound change and then quiet down.

"I bet it landed on Mirror Rock," said Johnny. "Want to go see it?"

"No. Let's stay here and watch," said Louise.

Just then a reporter and cameraman came over the trail from the top of the mountain and on down the trail toward the pine grove. "Hold on a minute," the reporter called to the work foreman. The other men had finished their task and were sliding down the path and climbing onto the pile of weeds in the back of the truck.

The foreman stopped and waited.

"I was hoping to talk to the boy who was responsible for the marijuana bust," called the reporter as he came closer.

"Right over there under the pine trees," shouted the foreman, pointing toward Johnny and Louise. Then he turned and slid down the trail himself.

When the cameraman was all set up, the reporter interviewed Johnny and Louise, asking them everything about how they found the patch, the arrest of Corn, and where they went to school.

Finally, they finished, and Louise and Johnny followed them back over the mountain and watched the helicopter take off. When the children got home after running back down the mountain, they were exhausted. Their morning had started very early, and Johnny flopped on his cot and promptly fell asleep.

The sound of a four-wheel-drive vehicle awakened him. As he pulled on his jeans, he heard Ma and Louise talking in excited voices on their way out. He hurried after them.

Outside, Johnny rubbed his eyes against the sunset's reflection on a shiny blue van. From it, Mr. Jenkins, Scott, and Sandy McRee stepped out.

"We've just come from your Uncle Elbert's store," Mr. Jenkins said to the children. "Your Pa offered to come up and get you, but we wanted to come, instead." He turned to Ma and said, "Your brother-in-law has planned a get-together at his store and..."

"*We're* invited, too," Scott cut in, "to see you and Louise on the big color TV set!" His brown eyes sparkled with excitement.

"Did you know you're celebrities?" Sandy asked Johnny and Louise.

Johnny smiled shyly. "I thought I was in big trouble. That's why I didn't tell them Scott was with me when I found that stuff growing in the pine grove."

Scott smiled and shook his head. "It doesn't matter one bit. I just feel real good about my friends getting on TV!"

"All the time, I was thinking Hank and Rusty planted it," Johnny admitted. "There was all them funny piles of leaves we saw at their cabin—" He clapped his hand over his mouth.

"Ummm-hummh!" Louise fixed him with a mischievous eye. He hoped she wouldn't tell Pa he had gone to the cabin.

"I met Hank and Rusty," Sandy said. "They're forestry students from Jimson University. They've been working on an assignment to try to find out how to save the mountaintop trees."

"We just happened to meet them at the foot of the mountain," Mr. Jenkins added. "We're to get together and map out some plans for the project to continue next year. If our mill is polluting the air and causing this, I intend to correct the problem. Also, Cougarville Textiles will sponsor their efforts."

"You said they'll work on it 'next year.' Ain't they gonna stay all winter?" Johnny asked.

"No," Sandy answered, "and your uncle has offered us the use of his cabin for church services. He says he'd like me to stay there overnight when I need a quiet place to study."

"How about that!" Johnny exclaimed. "Scott *said* it looked like a church."

"It won't be a bad place for me to tutor two young people who want to catch up on school work, either." Sandy's smile swept from Louise to Johnny, who tried a fast scowl before a big grin erased it.

"Are you folks ready?" Mr. Jenkins asked. "I left the rest of my family at the store. I need to get back before they buy more than I can haul home tonight."

"How about Aunt Lou?" Johnny asked.

"We stopped there on the way up," Sandy said. "We'll pick her up. She said she'd not miss this for anything."

Ma and Louise looked neat in freshly ironed jeans and plaid shirts that shouted the colors of autumn.

As they settled themselves in the back of the van, Louise smiled at her brother. "We got lots of special things on Mirror Mountain," she declared with pride in her voice. "I wouldn't want to live nowhere else."

Johnny stared at her for a moment, as though he couldn't believe what he'd just heard. "Comin' out of your mouth," he told his sister, "them words are somethin'."